"There you are," Ka[...] cheerfully, tucking a [...] hair behind a little sticky-out ear, not looking away from the screen inches from her face. "I was starting to wonder if you'd run away again."

"I told you to leave," Leander said roughly. Damn her. It had never occurred to him that she would stay after he'd spoken so cruelly to her. Anyone with an ounce of pride would have driven away cursing his name.

"For the sake of accuracy, you told me to see myself out. Now, I've messaged Helena with the good news that I've found you and updated her about your resistance to returning straight to Greece." She turned her head and fixed the heart-shaped face that reminded him of the pixies of folklore and eyes the color of jade at him with a steely smile. "I've promised to do everything I can to get you back there sooner rather than later—reading between the lines, your brother's being an arse—so consider me your houseguest until such time."

"Absolutely not."

The Forbidden Greek

MICHELLE SMART

HARLEQUIN

PRESENTS

PRESENTS™

Recycling programs for this product may not exist in your area.

ISBN-13: 978-1-335-59354-2

The Forbidden Greek

Copyright © 2024 by Michelle Smart

For questions and comments about the quality of this book, please contact us at CustomerService@Harlequin.com.

TM and ® are trademarks of Harlequin Enterprises ULC.

Harlequin Enterprises ULC
22 Adelaide St. West, 41st Floor
Toronto, Ontario M5H 4E3, Canada
www.Harlequin.com

Printed in Lithuania

MIX
Paper | Supporting responsible forestry
FSC® C021394

Michelle Smart's love affair with books started when she was a baby and would cuddle them in her cot. A voracious reader of all genres, she found her love of romance established when she stumbled across her first Harlequin book at the age of twelve. She's been reading them—and writing them—ever since. Michelle lives in Northamptonshire, England, with her husband and two young smarties.

Books by Michelle Smart

Harlequin Presents

Claiming His Baby at the Altar
Innocent's Wedding Day with the Italian
Christmas Baby with Her Ultra-Rich Boss
Cinderella's One-Night Baby

A Billion-Dollar Revenge

Bound by the Italian's "I Do"

Scandalous Royal Weddings

Crowning His Kidnapped Princess
Pregnant Innocent Behind the Veil
Rules of Their Royal Wedding Night

Visit the Author Profile page
at Harlequin.com for more titles.

For Pippa, who made our second collaboration
as much fun as the first xx

CHAPTER ONE

TRAVELLING BY PRIVATE jet was every bit as amazing as
Kate Hawkins had imagined. The cabin crew catered
to her every need and whim, serving her an array of
food that passengers on commercial airlines could only
dream of along with every possible drink her tastebuds could fancy, alcoholic and non-alcoholic alike.
She had her own lounge, a dining room, a bathroom
and even a bedroom with a mattress so comfortable
you'd have to be a world-class insomniac not to fall
into a dreamless sleep on it. Or too frazzled with the
task you'd volunteered yourself for to switch your brain
off enough to sleep.

In the space of thirty-eight hours Kate had travelled to seven different countries over two continents,
zipped through so many different time zones she'd no
idea if it was currently Sunday or Monday wherever
in the sky she was, and if Leander Liassidis wasn't to
be found at the next stop, there was a high probability
she would do more than stamp her feet and scream in
frustration like she'd done in Manhattan.

She pulled out the list Helena had written, the paper

now a crumpled, grubby mess, and stared moodily at the places still to be crossed off. How could one man own so *much*? Kate's property empire consisted of her childhood bedroom, which she'd moved back into full time after completing her veterinary degree two years ago. Leander, wildly successful technology tycoon worth billions, owned fourteen properties, and if it turned out he'd bought another one that Helena knew nothing of then there was an excellent chance Kate would throw herself out of the plane. Cabin fever had well and truly hit.

By the time it was politely requested that she buckle up for the landing, she couldn't be bothered to ask where the private airport they were flying into was located. All of Leander's properties were located within a thirty-minute drive of an airfield. She couldn't even be bothered to summon a glimmer of interest at the view as they descended of the Pacific Ocean lapping onto California's sandy shores. At least when descending over New York she'd grunted appreciation at the iconic skyline. Now her body clock was too shot to give a hoot.

'Grand Cayman next,' she said to her favourite of the crew with a weary smile as she left the plane. Kate was convinced she'd have to travel to every ruddy country listed before she found the runaway groom and dragged him back to Greece. The way she was feeling, she'd have to resist killing him. Maybe just settle for maiming him.

'We will await your call.'

As at all her previous stops, the efficient crew, who'd thus far organised everything, had arranged for a car to meet her at the foot of the plane. She had time to be grateful that she hadn't stepped into a furnace as she'd done in Manhattan before slumping into the back of it.

They hadn't left the airfield before her heavy eyes started fighting with her wired brain to stay open. Or was that to close? Images flickered in her retinas of the wedding, voices from it echoing in her head. The shock of seeing the wrong Liassidis twin waiting at the altar, the surrealness of hearing Leo recite his vows in Leander's name, time skipping to Helena, the beautiful bride, ashen faced with shock at what Leander had done, Kate's vow to find him and bring him back, of Leo giving her access to a company jet and...

Her eyes suddenly sprang open. She'd drifted into one of those vivid waking dreams and now found herself being driven through high trees on a road with No Trespassing signs displayed at intermittent intervals. High up in front of them loomed a huge glass-fronted property. As they drew closer, she saw that although framed by trees, the mansion faced the ocean. The driver glided to the smoothest of stops at the foot of a wide, curving path that led up to what she assumed was the main entrance.

Climbing out, Kate craned her neck upwards, trying to take it all in, trying to spot signs of life, waiting for the security guard that would appear at any moment and politely inform her that Mr Liassidis was not in residence and that he was unable to make contact with him because Mr Liassidis was on his honeymoon.

Mr Liassidis certainly was on his honeymoon. The only problem was, it was the wrong Mr Liassidis.

She supposed any of the security guards in Athens, Rome, Milan, Vienna, Frankfurt, London, New York and Toronto could have been lying to her but she hadn't sensed life behind those closed doors. Here though...

Exhausted legs dragging halfway up the path, she was just thinking that this was the most perfect of secluded hideaways when the requisite security guard appeared in front of her.

Leander Liassidis spotted the black four-wheel drive appear through the foliage and grimaced.

He supposed this meant his brother's minion had finally found him.

Hauling himself out of the pool, he rubbed a towel over his soaking body. He didn't need to tell Mason to send the visitor away. He'd already made his instructions explicit on this. Leander wasn't there. Leander was on his honeymoon. His visitor would leave Marina Sands empty-handed.

He briefly wondered how many of his properties the minion had visited to get this far. He could find out if he wanted but he was on a self-imposed communications blackout. Since satisfying himself that Leo had stepped up and taken his place, Leander hadn't wanted to know anything about the outside world.

For the first time in his life, Leander needed solitude. Outside his Californian household staff, whose loyalty and discretion was assured, only his PA knew his location. Sheree had been with him for ten years. Practiced at lying for him, her loyalty and discretion were also assured.

Slinging the towel around his shoulders, he popped the lid off a cold beer and drank a good slug of it. The bitter taste matched the way he felt towards himself for not going through with the wedding.

Leander loved Helena. An incredibly ugly baby who'd turned into an incredibly cute toddler and then a delightful child who'd followed him about like a puppy whenever their families had got together—which had been a lot, their families in business together and as close as if they were bound by blood—she was the one non-blood female constant in his life. She'd turned into a beautiful and smart woman, and he always looked forward to meeting up with her, adored being in her company. One thing he didn't have was any romantic inclinations towards her. Maybe it was over-familiarity, maybe it was because she was like a sister to him, whatever the reason, he'd never looked at Helena with the same eyes he looked at other women, and even if he had and even if it had been reciprocated—which it wasn't, being platonic ran both ways—he would never have acted on it for the simple reason that he loved her too much to hurt her.

And now he had hurt her. He'd broken his promise, and it tore his heart to think of the hurt and bewilderment that absconding the way he'd done must have caused her.

At some point in the near future he would return to his Greek homeland and face her, face his brother too, and step into the role of husband that he'd promised to play for her, but that point wasn't yet, and he downed the rest of his beer to drown the burn of bile in his throat at the thought of putting on a loving display to the world until Helena got her inheritance sorted and they could dissolve their sham marriage.

He *had* to get his head together.

Popping the lid off another beer, Leander settled his mind with the promise of spending the rest of the day getting rip-roaring drunk. About to head inside to shower, a lull in the ocean breeze carried the whisper of a voice up to him.

The hairs on the nape of his neck rose.

In four quick strides he was at the glass balustrade that overhung the path to his home.

Kate took one look at the security guard's face and pulled her own. 'Let me guess, Mr Liassidis isn't here?'

'Mr Liassidis is on…'

'His honeymoon,' she finished for him. 'And you are unable to contact him.'

'I'm sorry for your wasted journey.'

It was exactly what she'd expected, exactly what she'd experienced during her pitstops at Leander's other homes. And yet…

There was nothing in the security guard's demeanour or expression to make her think he was lying but something felt different, different enough for Kate to fold her arms over her stomach and flatly say, 'I don't believe you.'

'I can't help what you believe, ma'am, but Mr Liassidis isn't here and now I'm going to have to ask you to leave.'

She looked around him and up, trying to see through the glass that so effectively blocked the viewer from seeing anything of the beautiful home's interior.

'You need to leave now.'

Ignoring him, she continued scrutinising the exterior of what had to be the most spectacular home she'd ever seen.

'I must insist.'

'Must you?' she murmured absently. Kate's instincts were telling her loud and clear that the security guard was lying. Someone was resident in this house, she could feel it in her bones.

'Ma'am, I don't want to have to use force.'

That snapped her back to attention. 'Lay one finger on me and I'll sue you to kingdom come, got it?' Cupping her mouth, she shouted, 'I know you're in there, Leander Liassidis. Get your backside out here and stop hiding!'

'This is your last chance. You are trespassing. Either leave voluntarily or I carry you to your car. I can give you directions to the nearest law enforcement offices if you want.'

Her hands flew to her hips. 'What I *want*,' she

stressed, her patience stretched way past boiling point, 'is for your boss to stop hiding away like a big baby.'

'Mason, let her up.'

Kate's gaze shot back up to where the heavily accented gravelly voice had rumbled from.

There, hands gripping the darkened glass balustrade, stood Leander.

Energised vindication overrode her shock at his appearance, and she couldn't resist poking her tongue out at the security guard as she skipped past him. Moving as fast as her short legs would carry her, afraid the man she'd been sent on a wild goose chase to find would disappear as suddenly as he'd appeared, Kate wasn't sure if relief or fury was the strongest emotion raging through her. At least her instincts were working, so that was one plus. She'd *known* Leander was here the second she'd stepped out of the car. Known it, known it.

The top of the path led onto wide marble steps that fanned out, one side leading to the balcony, the other to the house itself. Leander had opened a section of the balustrade for her, and she steamed through it, more than ready to let rip at him. Except all the abuse she wanted to hurl suddenly tied itself on her tongue when she rounded to face him and was confronted with Leander wearing nothing but a pair of tight black swim shorts. The towel around his neck hardly covered any of him.

'Whoa!' Immediately she turned her back, scrunched her eyes closed and covered them with her hand for good measure. 'Put some clothes on, will you?'

'If my state of undress disturbs you, you know the way back to your car,' he said sardonically from behind her.

'I've just spent the best part of two whole days trying to hunt you down. I'm not going anywhere without you and you know it, so put some clothes on before I'm sick everywhere.'

She heard a put-upon sigh and then, 'You can look now. I am decent.'

'You're sure?'

'The floor tiling out here cost a fortune. I don't want it ruined with your vomit.'

Gingerly lowering her hand, Kate unscrewed her eyes and turned her head, only to immediately squeeze her eyes back shut. All he'd done was wrap the towel around his waist. 'That is *not* decent.'

'I didn't realise you were such a delicate flower.'

'Only when my eyes are bleeding.'

'Have you travelled all this way to insult me?'

Still keeping her back to him, she tightened her hold on her small handbag and imagined it was his neck. 'Leander, I'm moving to Borneo in a week and as you very well know, I've a million and one things I need to do before I go, so stop mucking about and put some ruddy clothes on. You'll need to be dressed for the flight back to Greece so do it now, otherwise you'll find I haven't even got started on the insults.'

There was a short but heavily loaded silence.

'How can I put this…? No.'

'What are you saying no to?' she asked indignantly.

She felt rather than heard him walk away.

'All of it,' he replied. 'I'm not going anywhere so why don't you save your breath and my ears and get back in your car, drive back to the airport, fly home, and start packing for your new life.'

Furious, she spun back around.

Leander had sat himself on one of the light grey L-shaped outdoor sofas that surrounded the swimming pool, both arms resting lazily along the back of it, a bottle of beer in hand, long tanned legs stretched out. He'd put a pair of shades on, his gaze fixed musingly at the sky as if judging what the weather planned to do. If Kate could command the weather she'd make it chuck it down with freezing rain on him.

'Well, I'm not going anywhere without you,' she snapped. 'I promised Helena and that brother of yours that I'd drag you back to Greece and that's what I'm going to do.'

'Tell that brother of mine that I'll return to Greece as promised before the honeymoon is over but it will be at a time of my own choosing, so fly away, little flower, and ruin someone else's day.'

'Nope.' Spotting an unopened bottle of beer in a bucket of ice on the table, Kate snatched it up and removed the lid with her teeth.

'Neat trick.'

'Isn't it?' She flopped onto the sofa closest to his and mimicked his pose, although keeping her gaze trained on his face. 'One of my brothers taught me that on my eighteenth birthday.'

'Sounds like my kind of guy. Go and ruin his day.'

'I've ruined many of my brothers' days over the years which means I've had *mucho* practice in annoying men, and now I'm going to stay here and annoy you until you give in and fly back to Greece with me.'

His jaw clenched but his gravelly voice retained the sardonic calm that had laced it since her arrival. 'Kate, go home. I'm not leaving.'

'I promised Helena I would drag you back,' she repeated stubbornly. 'And unlike *some* people, I don't break promises.'

'I told Leo I would be back before the honeymoon is over and I meant it.'

'Yes, I heard the message you left for him—aren't you lucky he heard it in time to take your place?' she retorted. 'You also told Helena you would be waiting at the altar for her. You *promised* her.'

The strong jaw clenched again. 'Leonidas stepped in for me.'

'Yes, and he is *not* happy about having to pretend to be you, and Helena is worried he'll pull the plug on the whole charade before the honeymoon's over, and you know what that means—if she's not married, she has to wait two more years for her inheritance, and she needs that money now.'

'Leo will not pull the plug.' He finally looked away from the sky and turned his shaded stare to her. 'Everyone should stop worrying. I will return before the honeymoon is over. No harm will have been done.'

'How can you say that with a straight face? Your

brother is furious, your parents are...' She shook her head. 'Actually, I don't know what your parents are thinking—they went along with the pretence but if you looked closely enough you could see their bewilderment, and as for Helena...'

'Helena got the marriage she wanted.'

'To the wrong brother! And the wrong brother is not a happy bunny. I get the feeling he likes Helena as much as you like me.'

'What do you mean by that?'

She laughed. 'Oh, come on, Leander. Don't pretend. I know you don't like me and you know I know because Helena asked what I'd done to offend you.'

In the almost fifteen years that Kate and Helena had been friends, Kate had heard a lot about Leander Liassidis but circumstances meant that until Kate had flown to the Liassidises' Greek island the week before the wedding, she'd never actually met him. She'd been looking forward to finally meeting the man Helena had always spoken so highly of, had been certain they would hit it off, and for the first days of their acquaintance her hopes had been realised. Leander was as fun, gregarious and charming as Helena had promised. On Kate's fifth night there, he'd flown the two English women to Athens for a night of food and dancing at an exclusive nightclub near his Athenian apartment. Kate had had the *best* time, and when they'd ended the night at his apartment, she'd been more than happy for the party to continue, the three of them and a handful of

Leander's friends drinking cocktails, downing shots and dancing until the sun woke up.

It had been early afternoon when she'd finally dragged her hungover body out of the gorgeous spare room she'd crashed—literally—in, and though it had to count as the worst hangover of her life, she'd still been buzzing from the fun they'd all shared. In many ways, it had been the celebration she hadn't even known she wanted, her chance to whoop it up and celebrate being just weeks away from starting her new life and the fulfilment of all the dreams she'd held since she was a little girl of seven.

She'd practically boogied into Leander's kitchen and had found him slumped over the kitchen island that was bigger than her bed. She couldn't remember exactly what she'd said but she'd cracked a joke about hangovers and when he'd lifted his head something had flickered on his face before he'd closed his eyes and in the gravelly voice that had up to that point been warm, icily said, 'I have a headache. I would appreciate some silence.'

Although stung at his unexpected coldness, she'd assumed it was his hangover talking and tried not to take it personally, expecting gregarious Leander to re-emerge soon enough. And he did. Gregarious Leander was fully back before they returned to the island...but not for Kate.

He didn't exactly blank her but there was something cool, almost dismissive about his new attitude to her. It had bugged her but it was only when she'd been sunbathing around the Liassidis pool the next afternoon, Helena having popped back to her room to get her portable phone charger, and Leander had appeared on the terrace, taken one look at her and, without a word, turned around and walked away, that she'd known he really had taken a dislike to her.

She'd mentioned it to Helena because it had bothered her and she'd worried she'd inadvertently done something to offend him. If she had, she would have apologised.

'You told Helena that you didn't have a problem with me but I'm not stupid, Leander, and quite frankly, I don't even care about your reasons any more. You need to—'

'I didn't want to hurt Helena with the truth but I'm more than happy to tell you my reasons for disliking you,' he cut in, removing his shades and fixing his dark brown eyes on her. 'You are like a buzzy bee in my ear.' He made a snappy gesture with his fingers and thumb for emphasis and leaned forwards. 'You don't know when to shut up and the stuff that comes out of your mouth is hardly worth the air you use to expel it. I can only assume you got someone to take your veterinary exams for you because you are a walking, talking template of the dumb blonde that people of our parents' generation used to make jokes about.'

He rose to his feet and, top lip curved in a sneer, added, 'Tell Helena and my brother I will be back before the honeymoon is over, as already promised. You can see yourself off my property.'

CHAPTER TWO

LEANDER'S BLOOD WAS still pumping hard as he washed his hair under the shower.

Of all the people his brother and Helena could have sent to track him down, why *her*?

Wiping the suds off his face with his hands, he wished he could wipe the look of shocked hurt on Kate's face from his eyes. Banish it.

It was for the best, he told himself as he lathered shower gel over his body. It had needed to be done. Kate couldn't be here.

He'd known Leo would send someone to find him because it was inconceivable he would take Leander at his word to come back. Leander had broken his word to his twin fourteen years ago and Leonidas had never forgiven him for it. Even though it had been five years since Leo had responded to any of his communications, Leander knew he could tell his brother it was raining and Leo would open a window to check for himself.

So yes, he'd expected Leo to send someone and demand he return to Greece immediately, and had prepared his staff accordingly. He would stay in seclusion until his head was together and his emotions under control, and only then would he return. A week was plenty of time to achieve all this.

But Leonidas and Helena had sent *her* to find him.

Why the hell had he revealed himself to her? It was a question still raging through his mind when he pulled a pair of heavy knee-length canvas shorts on. If he hadn't felt that strong compulsion to see if the voice was who every one of his senses had told him it was, Kate would have left Marina Sands in ignorance of how close she'd come to finding him.

He hoped like hell that she didn't take his cruel words to heart, but he'd needed to get rid of her and that had been the only way to achieve it.

Another sin he could add to his tally. The sin that cut the deepest. The most necessary of all his sins.

He needed to eat something. His usually healthy appetite had deserted him in recent days. It was almost lunch time and he hadn't eaten a thing, which for a man of six foot four was normally unthinkable.

He'd let his chef enjoy the balmy weather and make himself an omelette. Anything to do with eggs he could fix for himself. An omelette, a bucket of wine and a crap movie…

He stepped into his main living room and his plans dissolved in an instant.

Kate was on one of his sofas. Not just on it but stretched out, her head propped on a cushion, bare ankles hooked together below smooth, slender golden legs covered only to mid-thigh in khaki green shorts, busy doing something or nothing on her phone.

'There you are,' she said cheerfully, tucking a lock of blonde hair behind a little sticky-out ear, not looking away from the screen inches from her face. 'I was starting to wonder if you'd run away again.'

'I told you to leave,' he said roughly. Damn her. It had never occurred to him that she would stay after he'd spoken so cruelly to her. Anyone with an ounce of pride would have driven away cursing his name.

'For the sake of accuracy, you told me to see myself out. Now, I've messaged Helena with the good news that I've found you and updated her about your resistance to returning straight to Greece.' She turned her head and fixed the heart-shaped face that reminded him of the pixies of folklore and eyes the colour of jade on him with a steely smile. 'I've promised to do everything I can to get you back there sooner rather than later—reading between the lines, your brother's being an arse, which doesn't surprise me given everything Helen's told me about him—so consider me your houseguest until such time you agree to return.'

'Absolutely not.' He'd rather have radioactive cockroaches as houseguests.

'I'm afraid I only chucked a few bits of clothes in a bag when I set off to find you and I've left them in the plane, so I'll have to borrow some clothes off you, and also some toiletries and stuff—unless you don't mind having a stinky houseguest that is—and—'

Leander had never known a man's guts could clench

so tightly. 'This is all out of the question. You need to leave.'

'Can't.' Her smile widened. 'I've sent the driver away.'

'I'll get my driver to take you.'

'I'm not going anywhere without you, Leander, so unless you plan to physically throw me out of your home, you're going to have to put up with me annoying you and buzzing like a bee in your ear until you're so sick of me that you give in and do the decent thing and go back to Greece, and put Helena and Leo out of the misery you've inflicted on them.'

'How many times do I have to tell you, I will return to Greece before the honeymoon is over?' he demanded.

She turned her stare back to her phone and swiped at the screen. 'You can repeat yourself until you're blue in the face; no one trusts you to keep your word, and even if they did, this is supposed to be *your* honeymoon, and it's selfish of you to expect your brother to step away from all his responsibilities just because you can't cope with the idea of being tied to one woman without any sex for a few months at the most. If you need to get your leg over that badly, use some discretion. Helena won't care.'

'You think this is all about *sex*?' Swearing loudly, Leander paced the room, torn between doing exactly as Kate had said and throwing her over his shoulder to march her out of his home, and not wanting to even share the same air as her. The thought of touching her was too intolerable to contemplate.

'Well, you did tell your brother in that message you so kindly left him that something had come up, and you are known as Leander the Lothario,' she reminded him sweetly, 'so it does stand to reason.'

The tabloid moniker for him. It had never bothered him before. He'd actually found it quite useful. Women knew not to expect anything permanent from him. He could work hard and play hard without ties or responsibilities and enjoy his life and indulge in short but sweet successive flings without any expectations being levelled on him.

Kate attempted to keep her stare on the screen and not let it drift to Leander because she was still trying to banish the sight of him semi-naked from her retinas, which considering she'd sunbathed next to him numerous times—before he went all cold on her—and had barely paid his semi-nakedness the slightest bit of attention other than in a general *he's got a great body* way, was as disturbing as the pulses fluttering in her stomach.

'If it isn't about sex then what is it?' she asked when his only response was to glare malevolently at her. She couldn't see the glare but she could feel it. 'You told me only a week ago that you thought a fake marriage to Helena was *no big deal.*'

She'd asked him about it when they'd been sunbathing on her third day on his family island and Helena had been on a phone call. It had been Kate's first opportunity to grill him.

'What's in all this for you?' she'd asked, turning onto her side to face him.

He'd been lying on his back, fabulous body glistening under the searing sun, dark shades covering his eyes. He'd turned his face to her. 'You mean marrying Helena?'

'Yes. I know why she needs a quickie marriage and why she asked you—'

'Why was that?' he'd asked lazily.

'Because you're her second-best friend—'

'Only second?'

'Of course,' she'd grinned. 'I'm number one.'

White teeth had flashed.

'And she asked you because you have no ties and apparently no intention of ever marrying.'

'Oh, I might marry for real one day.'

'When you meet the right woman?' she'd teased, very much aware that Leander's playboy reputation was well deserved.

'That sounds remarkably romantic for a woman who wants to marry an orangutan,' he'd teased back, making her splutter with laughter. 'Life is for living, not being tied down, but I can see myself wanting children one day. If that happens, I might consider marriage, but it wouldn't be for a long time. Helena needs her inheritance now and the only way she can get it is by marrying, and as she won't accept money from me...' He'd flashed his teeth again. 'I just thought, why not?

It's no big deal for me. It'll be for a couple of months at the most. As soon as the inheritance is signed over to her, we will tragically go our separate ways.'

Kate's recollection of this conversation only made Leander's cold feet on the morning of the wedding even harder to understand. How could he be so blasé about it one day and then only days later flee thousands of miles? It just didn't make sense.

Leander could see from the way Kate had stilled that her clever brain was ticking and the clenching in his guts tightened to a point.

Folding his arms across his chest, it occurred to him that he could use that tabloid moniker and the reputation it had established to his advantage.

'You know what, Kate? You're right. This is all about my insatiable need for sex, and when I return to Greece, I'll be sure to tell Helena that I'll be taking lovers—discreet lovers, naturally—until she gets her inheritance and we can dissolve the marriage.'

She turned her face back to him brightly. 'Oh, good. Does that mean we can leave now?'

'You can leave whenever you want but I'm staying here. But seeing as you've put me in the mind for sex...' He gave her a meaningful stare.

Her nose wrinkled, just as he'd anticipated. Kate was the only woman he'd met in adulthood who gave no signs at all of desiring him. From Kate there had not been the slightest sign of awareness that she saw him as a man.

'God, you're disgusting.'

'Most women find me irresistible.'

'Then most women are stupid.'

He shrugged. 'If you won't oblige, my phone is packed with the names and numbers of women who would be happy to come over and satisfy my needs.'

Distaste written all over her face, she shrugged in return. 'Knock yourself out.'

'Some of my lovers have a tendency to be...how can I put this delicately?...vocal.'

She shrugged again. 'If they're too noisy I'll stick some cheese in my ears.'

How could she be so damned blasé? So unaffected?

Pulling his phone out of his back pocket, he waved it at her. 'Hundreds of obliging women.'

'Your mother must be very proud.'

'My mother understands me very well.' It was his identical twin who didn't. Or wouldn't.

Perching his backside on the side of the sofa next to Kate's head, glancing at the screen of her phone and seeing she was playing a word game which, for some reason added to his internal fury, Leander scrolled through his contacts. 'Who should I call? Grace? Hettie? Ah, Elle's in Santa Monica. That's not far. What do you think, Kate? Shall I call Elle? She's a real beauty.'

She tilted her head back to look up at him. The movement sent strands of her blonde hair brushing against his thigh. 'If you think Elle would be happy to be summoned to act as a vessel for your selfish pleasure, then by all means call her.'

'Stick around long enough and you'll find the pleasure is entirely mutual.'

'I'm sticking around until I get you back to Greece, even if it means using a whole block of cheese as ear plugs.'

He smiled cruelly down at her. 'I would suggest two blocks of cheese, and speaking of cheese, I'm hungry. If you're still planning to hang around where you're not wanted, you can make yourself useful and make me an omelette.'

'I'm happy exactly where I am, thanks.' And to prove it, she looked back at her phone and made another attempt to guess the day's word.

He laughed mockingly. 'You'll have to vacate your spot when Elle gets here—unless you want to watch as well as hear?'

Her mouth opened in a wide yawn she didn't bother to cover. 'I'm sure watching you have sex will be riveting.'

'I can go for hours.'

'Congratulations. You should add that to your email signature.'

'It's gauche to brag.' He got back to his feet. 'I'll call Elle now. I imagine she'll be here within the hour so if you see sense and decide not to ruin your dream job, dial one on the intercom and my driver will take you to the airfield. I'm going to make myself some food.'

'No onion in my omelette thanks.'

'If you want to eat, you'll have to go somewhere else. I will provide you with nothing.'

Unperturbed, she wiggled her toes. 'That's fine. I was a hungry student for five years, and besides, I'm sure the sight and sound of you having sex will kill my appetite for ever.'

Teeth clenched so tightly his jaw locked, Leander strode to his kitchen, more determined than ever to drive Kate Hawkins out of his sanctuary.

Kate waited until she was quite certain Leander wasn't planning to come straight back into the living room with another psychological attempt to make her leave before placing her phone on her chest, closing her eyes, and expelling a long breath.

She would not let his disdain for her affect her like he so obviously wanted it to. If he didn't like her and didn't want her in his home then tough luck. Kate had never broken a promise in her life and wasn't about to start now, especially not when that promise had been made to Helena. If not for Helena, she would never have survived boarding school and if she hadn't survived boarding school she'd have had to attend the local secondary school which was infamous for its lousy teaching and so would never have achieved the grades she needed to study to be a vet. She wouldn't be seven days from flying off to start her dream job, working at what was essentially a charity-run orangutan orphanage.

Kate had been one of only three full scholarship girls at her boarding school, one of the only girls who didn't spend the holidays in St Tropez or Klosters or wherever else Mummy and Daddy had a second or third or fourth home. The Hawkins annual family holiday was normally a fortnight in Spain or Portugal at an all-inclusive three-star resort which the other girls had all thought hilarious, and not in a good way.

Helena had been different. She hadn't cared that Kate's parents drove second-hand cars, lived in a semi-detached house and didn't have food delivered from Fortnum & Mason. Their friendship had been instant and had endured for almost fifteen years. As close as sisters, there was nothing they wouldn't do for the other, and if Helena needed Kate to cling like a limpet to Leander Liassidis until she could drag him back to Greece then she would forego any personal discomfort and do it. She knew exactly what was at stake for Helena if she failed and Leander's twin refused to carry out the pretence of being him any longer.

She didn't believe for a second that Leander would call Elle or any woman over. She had no idea where this certainty came from, but just as she'd instinctively known that he was in residence here, she also knew he was playing dirty psychological tricks to try and get rid of her, and she would swallow away her pride and the pangs that kept smashing into her chest that he made no bones about disliking her.

At least he was making it easier for her to despise him in return, and she would not allow herself any sadness that a man she'd struck such a great rapport with, someone she'd felt a real kernel of friendship unfold for, had turned out to be such a hateful bastard.

* * *

Leander's omelette looked pretty damn good, even if he did say so himself. Loaded with cheese and Serrano ham, he'd deliberately not put any onion in it, just to tantalise Kate's tastebuds. He would starve her out, and as he carried his plate out of the kitchen, he locked the door behind him. He'd never understood why the previous owner, an architect who'd designed the futuristic-looking mansion, had put locks on all the doors including the kitchen and now he could only assume they'd had a Kate invade their home.

Stopping at his floor-to-ceiling wine fridge, he selected a bottle of Chablis, plucked a glass from the cabinet beside it, and carried his haul into the living room.

The comment he'd planned to needle Kate with went unsaid when he crossed the threshold and found she'd fallen asleep.

He could do nothing to stop the swelling in his chest that rose all the way up his throat.

Still stretched out on her back, an arm had flopped down the side of the sofa, the tips of her fingers brushing against the rug on the floor. Her breathing was deep and rhythmic, the motions making the abandoned phone resting on her chest move and slide with each exhale.

Jaw clenched, he forced the swelling to subside and sat himself on a reclining armchair close to her. The aroma of cheese and ham would wake her up, he told himself, and if that didn't work, turning the television on and upping the volume would do the trick. Pressing the remote, the television sprang to life, a daytime home improvement show. About to increase the volume to eardrum bursting levels, he made the error of letting his eyes fall on Kate's sleeping face. The swelling set off again.

He'd been so intent on getting rid of her that he'd ignored the exhaustion lining her delicate pixie features.

He turned the television off and left the Chablis unopened.

Three bites of his omelette and he could stand it no longer. Putting his plate on the floor, he padded quietly over and gently removed the phone from her chest, being careful not to allow his fingers to make contact with the round-necked blue and white striped top she was wearing, and set it on the floor beside her sparkly flat sandals, close to the hand trailing on the rug.

The delicate fingers twitched.

His heart stopped.

Swallowing hard, he backed away and finished his solo meal.

The figure moved from the shadows of the door and stalked towards her, only a small towel hiding his nakedness. The closer he got, the more magnified his demonic beauty and the higher the thuds of anticipation in her chest. She couldn't open her mouth to speak but when his face hovered over hers, her lips parted. Threading her fingers into the black silk of his hair, she tightened her grip and moaned into the hungry possessiveness of his kiss...

Kate pulled herself out of the dream with a start. Eyes springing open, the deep blue of the crushed velvet sofa she'd fallen asleep on dominated her vision. Her heart was thumping so hard and so fast it was a burr against her ribs. If her hand wasn't already gripping her top she'd have to pat herself for assurance that she remained clothed.

It took an age before she found the courage to turn her head.

Leander was in an armchair reading, the strong jaw covered in thick black stubble set, the slightly too wide mouth compressed into a thin line.

'What time is it?' she mumbled, striving desperately to shake the dream and sleepiness off, and was more grateful than she could ever express that he didn't look up from his book when he answered.

'Seven.'

She'd slept for hours.

It took much more effort than it should to swing her feet to the floor. 'I need to use the bathroom.'

'I'm afraid the facilities here are unavailable for you.' His voice was as tight as his features.

That was better. Right then she needed him to be as mean as possible, to grow horns and develop cloven hooves.

'Fine. How about I pee on your rug?'

That made him look at her, and God did she wish he wouldn't, not until she'd scratched that dream from her memory for good.

The lips that had just kissed her in her dream pursing

in a put-upon motion, he nodded at the arch he'd gone through earlier, before she'd zonked out. 'First left.'

She crossed the vast living space, past the enormous central feature fireplace, and almost hoped he was sending her to a broom cupboard or something, just so she had something else to hate him for. But no, it was a bathroom, an ordinary downstairs bathroom with a toilet and a sink and which just happened to be one of the plushest downstairs loos she'd ever stepped in.

Only once she'd locked the door was she able to snatch a lungful of air.

Her heart was still racing when she washed her shaking hands with the deliciously scented hand wash and splashed cold water on her flushed face. It wasn't just her face that was flushed. Her insides felt liquidised.

God help her, that *dream*... It had felt so real.

She pulled more air into her lungs then ran her fingers through her mussed hair and rubbed away the last of the mascara applied over two days ago from under her eyes, forcefully reminding herself that it *hadn't* been real.

Even so, there was something frightening about her reflection, a feverishness she didn't recognise and which made her splash her face with more cold water.

One more deep breath and she left the bathroom.

Each step back to the living room made her heart race a little bit faster.

It was decidedly colder when Kate crossed the threshold. Most of the glass wall facing the ocean had been opened, cool evening air pouring in.

Leander's set profile was still focused on his book. He made no acknowledgement of her return.

The racing of her heart turned into a painful thunder. If she'd thought she could scorch the image of Leander's practically naked body from her retinas, her dream had put paid to that.

CHAPTER THREE

FILLING HER LUNGS deeply one more time for luck, Kate brought Helena's face to her mind. Helena was the reason why she was here, in the home of a man who couldn't stand her. Helena.

It had been a dream, that's all. A vivid dream but still just a dream. It didn't mean anything. She would shake it off and forget about it before the evening was done.

'I take it I missed Elle,' she said with determined breeziness as she reclaimed her spot on the sofa she knew perfectly well would be her bed for however long she ended up staying there. At least it was as comfortable as a real bed.

Leander didn't look up from his book. 'You missed all the fun.'

'She can't be that vocal if I slept through it all.'

'I doubt you'd have heard anything over the noise of your snores.'

'I don't snore.'

'How would you know? You were asleep. You sounded like a warthog.'

'You say the nicest things.'

A buzzer sounded from the ceiling.

He closed his book with a snap. 'That means my dinner is ready.'

'Don't let me hold you up.'

'Moussaka.'

She refused to let her expression change in the slightest. Kate had never tried the dish before her trip to the Liassidises' island and had fallen into raptures on her first taste. Leander had found this love for something that was so ordinary to him amusing, and they'd fallen into a long, detailed conversation about all their favourite foods.

'Try not to choke on it.'

'If I do, I'm sure you'll perform the Heimlich manoeuvre on me—after all, a dead Leander is no good for Helena, is he?'

'I'd be tempted to let you suffer a while first before saving you.'

'Then I'll make sure to chew thoroughly like a good boy.' With a tight, sarcastic smile, he disappeared from the vast room.

There was hardly the time for Kate to compose herself into a picture of serenity for he quickly returned carrying a tray with a plate heaped with an enormous mound of food and a gigantic glass of red wine.

'Not going to eat in your dining room?' she asked, affecting boredom.

'What kind of host would I be leaving my *guest* to her own devices while I eat?' He sat back on his armchair, took a drink of his wine and then took his first mouthful.

'Mmm…mmm,' he said appreciatively after he'd tried a sample of everything. 'You know, I think this might be even better than the moussaka we ate last week. And the lemon roasted potatoes…' He smacked his lips together and forked another mouthful in.

There was nothing Kate could do to stop her stomach from rumbling. It had to be a good sixteen hours since she'd last eaten. She was thirsty too, having not drunk anything since the beer she'd pilfered on the pool terrace.

The smile Leander gave proved without him having to say a word that he'd heard the rumble. He put his knife and fork on the plate, held a finger up to indicate he had something to tell her, then expertly held the tray with one hand as he stood and pulled a bottle of water from his shorts pocket.

'For you,' he said once he'd sat back down, and lobbed the bottle to her. 'Can't have my *guest* getting dehydrated.'

She caught it and smiled. 'Oh, you're just too kind.' Then she noted it was sparkling water. 'Just too kind,' she repeated, unscrewing the lid and putting it to her dry lips. Deliberately keeping her stare on his, she drank half the contents and tried not to let her aversion to the carbonated taste show on her face. Leander knew perfectly well that she hated sparkling water.

She watched him eat every last scrap, and when he'd finished and the empty plate was replaced with a pasta bowl of hot chocolate fudge pudding with whipped cream, she gave not the slightest reaction, not even when her stomach betrayed her hunger for the fourth time.

'There's a great restaurant two miles from here,' he confided as he steadily demolished a portion large enough to feed four people. 'It's in a cove and serves fresh seasonal seafood but it's the desserts it's famous around here for. They make a key lime pie that is out of this world.'

'Sounds great.'

'It is.' He pulled a face as if something had just occurred to him. 'You like key lime pie, don't you? I seem to remember you couldn't make up your mind what your favourite dessert is. Hot chocolate fudge cake with whipped cream or key lime pie.' He drank some more of his wine before holding up his glass. 'They also serve great wine. I'm told even the house red is palatable.'

'I'll be sure to pay it a visit if I ever return to this part of the world.'

'It closes at eleven if you want to try it now.'

'I'm good,' she said, even as her stomach betrayed her yet again.

His smile was knowing. 'Most Marina Sands' restaurants stop serving food by ten but there's a couple of twenty-four-hour drive-throughs on the outskirts. I've heard one of them serves food that doesn't taste like cardboard. I'm quite sure they all sell still water too.'

She pulled a shocked face. 'Still water? Wow. That's certainly something for me to think on.'

'My driver is at your disposal. Dial one on the intercom and you will be taken anywhere you wish to go.' His dessert finished with, he disappeared again, this time returning with a coffee that smelt so good Kate had to clench her buttocks to stop herself from jumping off the sofa to snatch it out of his hand.

Revenge was soon hers when Leander reclined his chair and turned the television on and found a film clearly designed to bore as it was a spy thriller without any thrills, and she proceeded to annoy him by chattering away about everything from the protagonist's impractical shoes to the implausibility of the plot line, not giving her mouth a rest long enough for him to take any of it in.

He thought she was annoying? Well she was delighted to prove just how annoying she could be.

It took less than thirty minutes for him to jump up from his recliner and announce he was going to take a walk on the beach.

'Sounds like fun,' she immediately enthused. 'I'll join you...' And then she caught the glint in his eyes and instinct told her that the moment she left the glass walls of his home, all the doors would be locked to her. 'Actually, I think I'll stay here.'

His smile as tight as his clenched jaw, he walked out without another word and disappeared into the darkness.

Leander filled his lungs with the salty ocean air and cursed himself for not thinking to put shoes on. Or a sweater. The breeze from the ocean kept the daytime temperatures in Marina Sands temperate all year round but the evenings were often much cooler. When he stepped onto the sand at the foot of his private path to the beach, his toes curled in protest.

He supposed it was a good thing Kate had resisted walking the beach with him. The temptation to throw her into the ocean might have proved too much. To throw her into the ocean would have meant having to touch her, and a memory flashed of her dancing in his Athenian apartment, one hand clutching a cocktail, the other waving above her head as she sang along loudly to the track playing, and Dimitri sidling up to slip a hand around her waist and palm her flat stomach over her pretty summery dress, Kate's scream of laughter and—

Leander upped his pace.

She'd be gone soon, he told himself grimly. He'd locked all the rooms so she was confined to the main living room which turned chilly overnight and all she had to wear were those shorts and that top that only reached her elbows. Opening the external doors had already driven out the residual heat. She was already hungry. Come the morning—if she lasted that long— she'd be freezing and starving. Even Kate, with all her tenacity and stubbornness, would have to admit defeat and leave.

By the time Kate figured out how to close the external doors of the living room that was twice the size of her parents' entire home, all the warmth had escaped. A search of the house for something warm to drape over herself ended in failure. Of the internal doors, only the downstairs bathroom was unlocked. The only fabric she'd found to warm herself with was the hand towel in the bathroom.

Back in the living room, she had another look at the central fireplace. Stumped at how to turn it on, she called out for Leander's staff—she knew there had to be staff around seeing as his dinner hadn't cooked itself. Her shouts went unanswered so she dialled one on the intercom. It was answered before the first ring had finished.

'Where would you like me to take you?' a feminine voice on the other end of the line asked.

'Actually, I was hoping you or another member of staff could turn the fire on for me,' Kate said. 'It's freezing in here.'

'I'm sorry, ma'am, but I'm not authorised to do that. I am only authorised to drive you to any destination of your choice.'

'Would you drive me to England?'

'If that's what you asked of me. It might take some ingenuity to manage it but I would do my best.'

'So you can drive me to England but can't turn the fire on?'

'I'm sorry, ma'am, but we have our instructions.'

Kate sighed. 'Thanks anyway.'

Ramming her hands into her shorts pockets, she took stock. She was cold and hungry but not defeated. For all Leander's bull-headed determination, her very presence was an aggravation to him. And the good thing about being cold meant the heat of her dream had finally disappeared.

She just wished the dream itself would vanish. Forget the current circumstances and the not insignificant fact that he couldn't stand her, she had no right allowing Leander into her dreams. He was as off-limits as off-limits could be and it didn't matter that Helena had no romantic feelings towards him or that their marriage was a sham and probably not even legal considering the wrong twin had made the vows and signed the certificate; in Kate's mind he belonged to Helena.

In her almost twenty-six years on this earth, Kate had never dreamt about a man, not even Euan, her two-week university fling that hadn't even been a real fling but which she'd ended abruptly when—

Outside lights came on.

Heart suddenly thumping, she hurried back to her original sofa and curled up on it, warming her feet as best she could under her bottom, and turned her phone on.

The glass door slid open.

Her heart thumped harder.

Leander's gaze zoomed straight to her. The instant his dark brown eyes locked onto hers, Kate's thumping heart stopped and her breath caught in her throat.

Barely moments passed before her heart kick-started itself with a roar, sending hot blood pounding in every direction.

A slow blink and then Leander's huge shoulders

rose and a tight smile pulled against his set features. 'Still here I see.'

She had no idea how she was able to summon a quip through the loud pulsing in her ears. 'Your powers of observation are astounding.'

'Nearly as astounding as your capacity for self-torture.' He slid the door shut. 'I'll keep this unlocked so you can see yourself out. I'm going to bed.'

'Not going to call one of your pleasure vessels to keep you company?' She had no idea where that remark came from either, knew only that it was a remark that should have gone unsaid because the last thing she wanted to think or talk about in that moment was Leander having sex, not when she was already feeling so…*aware* of him. Her only comfort was that her tone had been pithy rather than bitchy.

The tight smile pulled a tiny bit wider. 'The call's already been made. I'll keep my bedroom door open so you can watch.' The sensual lips pulled wider still. 'If you get too cold my bed's big enough for three.'

Even though she knew this was just another mind game that she'd been stupid enough to leave an open goal for him to score in, a hot flush crawled through her, enflaming her bones, her skin…enflaming *everything*.

Somehow she managed to retain the pithiness to say, 'I'm sure I'd much rather freeze.'

'A night in here without the heating on and no blankets and you will do just that.' The smile dropped. 'Remember, dial one on the intercom and my driver will take you anywhere you want to go.'

It had been many years since Leander had gone to bed so early and the first time he'd slid under the blankets with fury snaking through his veins. Anger was only ever a fleeting emotion in him. His twin held onto it enough for them both. Leander had been the one to cut the invisible umbilical cord conjoining them as identical twins but Leo had been the one to sever it in its entirety. For five years Leo had acted as if he had no brother, every message Leander had sent him remaining unanswered, although not unread. He hadn't even RSVP'd the wedding invitation.

Leander had known though, that Leo would never refuse a direct request for help just as he would be unable to refuse Leo if the roles were reversed.

Theós, it had been surreal hearing his own voice down the end of the line after so long, even if it was only a short invitation for the caller to leave a message.

At the time he'd made the call, Leander's only thought had been getting as far from Greece as quickly as possible, but since then he'd thought of his brother more than he'd done in years. He'd kept tabs on him through family and news reports just as he knew Leo kept tabs on him, but he hadn't consciously thought about him. If he was being truthful, he'd actively avoided thinking about Leo. To think of his twin was to acknowledge the wound in his heart.

When he'd told Leo his decision all those years ago

he'd known it would hurt him. He would have hurt too if the roles had been reversed. What he'd had no way of knowing was that things would deteriorate so badly and culminate with Leo cutting him from his life.

All of Leander's thoughts during that first contact in five years had been clouded by the woman currently sleeping on the ground floor below his bedroom. She couldn't know it but the sofa she'd made herself at home on lay directly beneath his bed.

Damn her. Damn her for treating her invasion of his home as one big game. Damn her for being so… *Kate*.

His wired brain refused to shut down. His heart refused to settle into a natural rhythm. His unwanted houseguest refused to remove herself from his mind's eye.

Midnight chimed and she was still there.

How could she be so stubborn? If she didn't leave soon she was going to give herself hypothermia.

He turned over and angrily punched his pillow. So what if she gave herself hypothermia? It would be her own damn fault. He'd given her every means to leave. One call and she could be driven in a heated car to a drive-through and then on to the airfield. There was no need for her to put herself through this unnecessary suffering.

Kate had huddled as deep into the sofa as she could go, knees hugged into her chest. The hand towel was draped over her feet but still goosebumps scored her flesh. She couldn't stop shivering. So cold was she that even the hunger pangs had gone into hibernation.

At least she wasn't thirsty. After leaving the living room, Leander had returned with two bottles of water for her, which he'd placed silently onto a sideboard before disappearing again without looking at her. Naturally, they were sparkling water.

As much as it pained her to admit it, she didn't think she could endure this for much longer. It was two a.m. and despite her long sleep that afternoon, she was still exhausted but sleep refused to come. She was just too cold. There were hours more to suffer before the sun rose and warmed the vast room.

But it wasn't just the coldness driving sleep away and making the thought of pressing one on the intercom ever more tempting.

Her brain was torturing her too.

Every time Kate closed her eyes the terrible dream was right there, dancing before her eyes, making her pulses accelerate and a terrible fever break out on her freezing skin. The deeper her exhaustion, the worse it all got, and her only successful attempts at driving the dream away were a failure of a kind because to replace them her mind filled with memories of all the fun and laughter they'd shared before he'd turned against her.

What had she done to provoke the change? In the stillness of the cold night, it was the one question that loomed larger than anything.

She must have done *something* because, for all his talk of her being an annoyance, his coldness had been too sudden for that excuse to be credible. Her last concrete memory of Leander and that night in Athens was shimmying over to where he was making cocktails. Leander had shimmied with her, shaking the cocktail maker in time to the beats pumping loudly through the whole apartment, the joy of good music and the excellent atmosphere flowing between them, and then he'd filled a glass with his creation and passed it to her with a mock bow. She'd shimmied away, blowing him a kiss that he'd caught with a huge grin and slapped to his stubbly cheek. Barely ten hours later she'd found him slumped over his kitchen island and he'd been cold with her ever since.

Leander punched his pillow for what had to be the fifteenth time and then something in him snapped.

Throwing the duvet off, he stormed down the winding stairs and into the living room.

Kate must have heard the heavy tread of his angry feet because he could see through the silvery light dancing through the windows that she'd lifted her head.

'Do you have some kind of damned death wish?' he demanded as he slammed his hand against the switch that turned on the soft up-lights rather than the main lights that would have blinded them both.

Immediately she turned her face into the sofa with the rest of her curled-up body. She was pressed so tightly into it she was close to being a part of it, but it was the small hand-towel wrapped around her feet that ripped through him the hardest.

'Why won't you leave?' he shouted into the unnerving silence. 'Why put yourself through this? What are you trying to prove? Do you think giving yourself hypothermia is going to make me soften and let you stay? Do you think Helena would want you to make yourself ill for her sake?'

But still she didn't answer. Still she kept her stubborn little back turned to him.

Cursing in Greek at her sheer bloody-mindedness, Leander stormed back up the stairs.

Kate heard a distant door slam and stuffed her fist into her mouth to stifle the sob that wanted to break free.

She'd wanted to shout back at him, remind him of the promise she'd made to Helena but her heart had been pounding so hard the beats had rippled in her throat.

It was seeing him emerge from the darkness that had set the reactions off. The silvery light had magnified his demonic beauty. Just like in her dream. He'd been wearing only a pair of boxer shorts, as little as he'd been wearing in her dream.

But in her dream he hadn't used his mouth to be cruel to her.

She took a long shuddery breath and turned over. Annoying Leander into submission was one thing but the way he'd just shouted at her...

She'd been right that his attitude towards her ran deeper than mere annoyance, but she'd underestimated the depths to which his dislike had reached.

Leander didn't just dislike her. He *hated* her.

What had felt, in part, like a game, a battle of wills between them, now tasted very different under the weight of his visceral loathing.

Heavy footsteps crashed back down the stairs.

If his demonic beauty had struck her dumb before, now it was the bundle he held in his arms.

He dumped it on the end of her sofa, snatched the top item and threw it onto her lap. 'Put this on,' he said roughly.

It was a black long-sleeved brushed cotton top.

He pressed his huge hand onto the rest of the bundle. 'Duvet and pillow. I'll leave you to make yourself comfortable.'

He stalked across the living room and disappeared.

Stunned at the unexpected gesture, Kate spent an age gazing at the duvet and pillow until her shivering flesh forced her into action.

Shaking the duvet out…oh, it was so wonderful and heavy…she hauled it over herself then stuck the pillow where her head rested and slipped the lounging top over her head. It smelt of fabric softener. It smelt clean.

Lying down, she huddled under the heavenly duvet and, while she waited for her body to accept the warmth and defrost, became aware for the first time that her bra was digging into her shoulders and ribs, and the button of her shorts was pressing into her belly.

Sitting back up, she took the lounging top and her own top off, then, while keeping the duvet around her shoulders for warmth by trapping it beneath her chin, unclasped her bra. The relief was so immediate that she wondered how she hadn't noticed the pain it had been causing her before. With the duvet still trapped between her chin and neck, she slid the straps off and scrambled again for the clean lounging top. There was a shock of cold against her breasts when she released the duvet to pull the top over her head and it flumped down to her waist, but then, once her arms were in, tugged it down, untucked her trapped hair and…

And noticed Leander as still as a statue by the fireplace, holding a crystal tumbler filled with a dark liquid.

Suddenly Kate found she didn't need the top or duvet for warmth. The flush that crawled through every inch of her was hot enough to generate heat for the whole of Marina Sands.

Time stood suspended. She couldn't drag her stare from Leander, could do nothing to stop the flush deepening and pulsing as the perfectly sculpted tanned torso fully etched itself into her paralysed brain, all the tiny details she'd never allowed herself to acknowledge before, from the dark hair covering the defined pecs and washboard abdomen to the indentation of his navel. All the tiny details that saturated her heated brain even while her eyes remained trapped in his stare.

His throat moved—how had she never noticed how strong it was before?—and his shoulders—broader than she'd ever recognised—lifted before his strong Roman nose flared and his lips compressed into a line so tight they disappeared.

A moment later he crossed the room to the archway that led to the stairs and the whole of him disappeared.

CHAPTER FOUR

LEANDER DRANK HIS Scotch in one huge gulp.

His skin had never felt so tight. The beats of his heart had never drummed so loudly in his ears.

God help him, Kate's breasts...

He gritted his teeth.

It had no effect.

God, they were every bit as beautiful as he'd refused to allow his mind to imagine. More so. Fuller than her petite frame suggested. Nipples the colour of dusky rose...

A groan rose up his throat.

He'd never experienced such painful arousal before.

He needed a shower.

Setting the temperature as low as he could withstand, Leander stood beneath the cold spray and willed the unwanted arousal to abate. If it was only in his loins he could have handled it, relieved himself and be done with it, but this was everywhere. Every cell in his body. Every cell begging for one little taste but one little taste would never be...

God damn it, why had he allowed himself to soften

enough to strip a spare bed for her? Telling himself that it wasn't the same as inviting her to sleep in the spare bed cut no ice. The only reason he hadn't invited her to use it was because he couldn't endure Kate sleeping on the same floor as him. Bad enough knowing she was curled on the sofa he doubted he would ever use again. He would throw it out. Replace it.

And what had possessed him to give her an item of his own clothing? If he'd resisted, she would never have thought to take her clothes off and he would never have seen...

He squeezed his eyes as tightly shut as he could manage to eradicate the image of her breasts from his mind, but all he succeeded in doing was replacing them with the look that had slowly crept over her face in those moments when he'd been unable to tear his gaze away from her.

It was a variant of a look he'd seen so many times that he hardly noticed it any more. But he'd never seen it on Kate's face before and it made everything a thousand times worse.

Leander beat the sun up. He'd had little sleep, his brain too wired at the presence of the woman haunting his home to fully shut down. Before his eyes opened, the memory of Kate's naked breasts and the feel of that look that had passed between them hit him with vivid colour and he was wide awake in an instant, painfully aware only the floor beneath his bed separated them.

He needed to hit the surf. Once he'd driven out the

angst that had his guts clenching so tightly and his pulses beating so strongly he'd be in a better frame of mind to up his game and force her from his home. If that look should pass between them again...

He descended the stairs quietly, intending to leave through the utility room, but before he could stop himself, he stepped into what had quickly turned into Kate's domain.

She was turned away from him, curled into the sofa fast asleep.

The churning in his stomach was violent enough to induce nausea.

Turning on his heel, he slipped back out of the room.

Kate's eyes pinged open. Although crushed blue velvet lay in her immediate vision, it was Leander she saw, his expression in that terrible, terrible moment that had passed between them, the complete stillness that had quickly morphed into disgust.

It was an expression that had made anything more than snatches of sleep impossible. She had the awful sense she would remember it for the rest of her life.

Being an annoyance she could handle, but being hated? That cut deeper than she could have believed. She'd never been hated before, not even by the snobby boarding school girls who'd taken cruel delight in patronising and mocking her, and to experience that hatred from the charming, fun, attentive man who'd made her laugh so hard and whose company she'd revelled in...

It didn't help that she'd developed this awful awareness of him that didn't seem in any hurry to shake itself off. During their week on his family's island, when the two of them and Helena had spent almost all their time together, Kate had acknowledged Leander was a hunk, mainly because she wasn't blind, but his hunkiness had had no effect on her.

Whatever protective layer had been on her eyes and mind in Greece, being alone with him here had stripped it away. The dream had ignited it and switched her awareness on. One little dream. One little dream that had roused something in her, awakened her to the fact that Leander wasn't just a hunk of a man but the most rampantly sexy man alive.

Rolling over, she squeezed her eyes shut in an attempt to eradicate the disgust on his face from her retinas, then swung her feet to the floor and rubbed her temples.

She needed to pull her big-girl knickers up and think practically. Her mission was to drag Leander back to Greece before his brother pulled the plug on the whole thing, and in good time for Kate to return to England and make the final preparations needed before she flew off to start the new life she'd worked so hard for. Leander's wild success in life and the way he'd treated her since her arrival here suggested he had an ever-flowing tap of ruthlessness, but she was stubborn, and her love and loyalty for Helena meant she'd wear him down before he broke her spirit. Admittedly, she needed to find a new approach to wear him down with, but so long as she kept her focus on the mission in hand and ignored all the terrible things happening inside her, she would complete it successfully.

Feeling clearer in mind if not in body, Kate headed to the downstairs bathroom. Her heart jumped to find a toothbrush and toothpaste on the ledge above the sink.

She stared at the two items, absently rubbing her bottom lip as her brain raced at all the possible meanings behind it. Was Leander softening? Feeling guilt? Had he caught a whiff of her breath and decided this was the one amenity he would provide? Had it even come from him? Had a member of his invisible staff put it there out of concern for Kate's oral hygiene?

No point wondering about it, she decided, and spread the minty paste over the brush.

Once she'd scrubbed her teeth and cleaned the rest of herself as best she could with only hand wash and a hand towel to use, she returned to the living room, lighter in heart than she'd been since waking from the dream.

Padding to the glass wall, she pressed her forehead to it and gazed out. The rustling of the trees and the movement of the ocean suggested a strong breeze and she felt a sudden yearning to stand out in it.

There was the same stillness to the house she'd felt when Leander had taken his walk on the beach, and on impulse she slid the glass wall open and stepped onto the terrace.

For long seconds she stood just past the threshold, alert to any sound, half expecting a member of his staff to come pouncing out to slam the door behind her, but the stillness behind her remained.

The ocean was the opposite to still, and when she moved tentatively to the balustrade to look out over it, Kate spotted a surfer riding what seemed to her untrained eyes as humungous waves.

It was the sigh of her heart that told her who the surfer was, a sigh that came after she'd spent Lord knew how long watching him, transfixed. It was a sigh that leapt up and stuck in her throat when he seemed to both ride and race a wave that continued to grow and had to be tens of metres high until the wave peaked and the surf swallowed him whole.

A puppy-like whimper sounded from her throat. The only movement her frozen body was capable of making was the tightening of her knuckles.

The thumping in her chest when he finally reappeared, feet secure on the board, knees bent, arms stretched out, still surfing that wave as it pounded onto the beach, was powerful enough to weaken Kate's legs.

Almost dizzy with relief, it took a long moment to register that he'd jumped off the board and was carrying it onto the beach…and that his gaze was fixed in her direction.

Kate didn't get the chance to act on her new, admittedly undecided, approach to her mission because for the whole of the day she was left entirely alone.

Leander had returned from his morning surf through

an entrance that kept him out of her sight. He'd been out of her sight ever since.

But not out of her mind. She didn't know when but at some point Leander or one of his staff had removed the remote controls for the television, and now her phone's battery was close to death and she'd left the charger on the plane. With nothing to occupy her mind, it filled itself with Leander.

Hours she spent at the glass wall gazing out over the ocean, watching too the surrounding foliage sway in the strengthening wind. He wasn't out there in it. He was here, under the same roof as her, avoiding her as if she were a carrier of the plague.

As a tactic to wear her spirits down, it was an effective one. Kate wasn't used to having only her thoughts for company. She was used to her brain being continuously occupied and used to background noise, whether the noise of her family, her university housemates, or Helena and the general noise of an all-girls school. She'd long ago learnt the art of blocking out sounds so she could concentrate on her studies, but today there was no noise to block and nothing to fill her mind but the man actively shunning her, making her question again and again what she could have done to turn him against her so completely.

Memories of their days together on his island played continually in her mind, the two of them and Helena, carefree days Kate had known even as she'd been living them that she would one day look back on as some of the best days of her life. Leander had made those days special. Leander just being Leander.

Where was that man now? Not the physical body he was wrapped in but the fun, gregarious, surprisingly thoughtful man beneath the skin? Just what had she *done* to drive him away?

It was only the silence of her own company that meant she recognised his nearing footsteps long after the sun went down and enabled her to force her features into a version of nonchalance. If he could see beneath her skin he'd see the nonchalance was nothing but a front. At the first sight of him, crystal glass filled with what looked like Scotch or whisky in hand, her pulses surged.

The casual attire she'd always seen him in had been replaced with a suave dark grey suit that her inexpert eye knew had been tailored especially for his huge frame. The large collar of the crisp white shirt was opened at the throat, the contrast in colour highlighting the deep bronze of his skin. The black stubble on his face had been trimmed, his hair styled.

The scent of freshly showered Leander topped with carefully applied cologne filled the space surrounding them. It was a scent that threw her back what felt a lifetime ago but was in reality not even a week, to when she'd climbed into the helicopter transporting them to Athens and she'd inhaled this exact same scent, and chirpily said, 'Ooh, you smell nice.'

He'd grinned. 'Better than the orangutan you're going to marry.'

Kate's heart throbbed to remember that little exchange and remember the light, teasing nature of the friendship that had sprung up between them.

The easy smile that had never been far from the surface...no hint of it now. No hint of it for her since Athens. What had she *done*?

Lips compressed into a thin line, hard dark eyes fixed on her, he raised his hand and took a drink of his liquor. The movement exposed the fine black hairs on his wrist. For some inexplicable reason, seeing those hairs only tightened the throbs of her heart.

For all the hardness of his features, his gravelly voice was as smooth as silk when he said, 'I'm going out.'

Although she'd registered that Leander was dressed for a night out, it hadn't been a conscious thought, and she had no idea why it felt like a fist had wrapped itself around her throbbing heart. She cleared her throat and uttered her first word that whole day. 'Where?'

'That is none of your business.'

'But you can't.' She tried to think coherently through her wildly scattering thoughts. Was he leaving his bolt hole because of her? Did he hate her *that* much? 'You'll be seen.'

Leander shrugged and drank some more of what was his third glass of Scotch that early evening. 'No one knows me here. In Marina Sands, I'm just another rich guy who likes to surf.'

And even if people did know him here in this little pocket of California, it was a risk he would be willing to take because he could not stand another damned minute trying to kid himself that slender, pixie-faced Kate Hawkins with the dancing jade eyes wasn't ensconced in his living room, pacing the walls he'd confined her to, hungry...

Her hunger was her own fault. She wasn't a guest. She was lucky he was providing her with water. She could leave at any time of her choosing.

And so could he.

There was no risk in what he was doing. He'd chosen Marina Sands for its surfing and the ocean view. If anyone from his world should happen to be in a bar in a town so insignificant its name was barely known to anyone outside the immediate vicinity, they would assume he was Leo. That would be the natural assumption because anyone who'd even touched his social circle knew Leander Liassidis was on his honeymoon. The foulness of his mood meant he could pass himself off as Leo without any effort at all.

Driven out of his own home by a woman half his size.

Or should that be driven out of his own home because the woman half his size was driving him out of his mind? He must have been out of his mind to instruct his staff to arrange toothpaste for her. He shouldn't care if she got cavities. Any good done by his morning surf, cut short by the gusty winds, had gone to hell when he'd looked up and found her staring at him from the balcony.

With the weather as foul as his mood, he'd resorted to spending the day in his gym, working on every piece of equipment to distract himself from the infuriating woman who just didn't know when to quit. He couldn't even throw himself into work as a distraction because he was supposed to be on his damned honeymoon.

Damn Kate Hawkins and her dancing jade eyes for not having the grace to get the hell out of the sanctuary he'd escaped to.

Those jade eyes weren't dancing now. She was ten feet away from him but even that distance wasn't far enough to hide the emotion flashing from them.

The only person who'd ever looked at him with anything even close to that kind of emotion was his twin.

He turned his gaze from her.

'But…what if you *are* recognised?'

'This isn't a debate,' he said icily, finishing his Scotch. Forget going to a bar. He would call his flight crew and disappear again. He should have done that the moment he realised Kate was prepared to hunker down for as long as it took to drag him back to Helena. 'I am informing you of my plans as a matter of courtesy and so I can remind you that, should your few brain cells finally recognise you're in a no-win situation here, all you have to do is—'

A tiny body flew at him, a small hand gripping his wrist before he could finish repeating his mantra about the intercom.

She'd moved so quickly he'd barely had time to register her legs moving.

'Why are you being so cruel to me? What did I do to make you hate me so much?' she demanded angrily.

Caught off guard by the speed with which she'd flown at him, completely unprepared for her beautiful pixie face to be so close that he could see the swirling hues of her eyes currently firing hurt and anger at him, it was as much as Leander could manage to grit out, 'Let go.'

Her features were taut, her breathing ragged. 'Not until you tell me what I did.'

Fixing his sight on an abstract painting, he said through a jaw clenched so tight it felt in danger of snapping, 'Let go of my wrist, Kate. I will not tell you again.'

Her grip only tightened. 'You could easily move my hand if you wanted to but you won't touch me, will you? You won't even look at me. I've got a ton of photos on my phone of you smiling and laughing with me, and now you can't even bring yourself to look at me. For the love of God, tell me, *what did I do?*'

'You did nothing,' he dragged out. The blood pumping through him felt like fire. The torturous heat of her grip was spreading like wildfire through his blazer and shirt, burrowing beneath his skin and into his veins.

'If you're going to tell a barefaced lie at least have the courtesy to look me in the eye while you tell it,' she cried, and it was the underlying pain in her voice that snapped his stare back on her. 'We were *friends*, Leander. Those days we spent together were some of the best of my life. You went out of your way to make me feel welcome and accepted in your family's home, and you included me in *everything*. You looked out for me too—you insisted on escorting me to the ladies' room in that nightclub in Athens so I didn't get harassed by drunken men for heaven's sake, so don't tell me I didn't do anything when...'

Kate's emotional onslaught came to an abrupt end when Leander twisted his wrist from her grasp and captured her face in his hands.

Suddenly pressed against the sideboard, her demonic tormentor's face loomed over her, all coldness gone, his dark eyes staring intently into hers as if he were preparing to bite her head off in one snap.

'You did *nothing*,' he repeated harshly...but the harshness was counteracted by the molten intensity of his stare as his face drew nearer and his voice lowered to a husky, 'except be you.'

Kate's chest filled. Trapped in his molten stare, her pulses thrashed wildly, her senses springing to life as Leander's heat and scent engulfed her.

He pressed closer to her. Her breasts brushed against his chest. The floor beneath her feet shifted into sand.

She was sinking...

Their faces were so close she could feel his breath on her mouth...

Something guttural came from his throat and he abruptly dropped his hold on her cheeks.

In the blink of an eye the heat of his body vanished and in the blink of an eye that it took for her confused body to feel the loss of it, he strode to the sliding wall.

It took a few moments for the hot blood whooshing

in Kate's head to clear enough for her brain to reengage with her body.

Running after him, she darted out onto the balcony. Leander's silhouette had already reached the section of the balustrade that opened onto the pathway.

'What do you mean, *except be you*?' she shouted over the now howling wind.

The silhouette went through the gate. It slammed shut behind him.

'Leander!' She was all fingers and thumbs with the latch of the glass gate, and in frustration she kicked it with her bare foot.

He was halfway down the path by the time she opened it, yelling out his name but finding it lost in the noise of the strengthening storm. But he heard her, she knew it with the same certainty that she'd known he was in residence when she'd first walked this path.

Whether it was the smarting pain in her toe from kicking the gate or the awful, awful emotions raging through her or her inability to wrench her stare from Leander's rapidly retreating figure that stopped her watching where she was walking…running…but as she chased after him, shouting out his name, she missed a shallow step. Losing her footing, she went sprawling.

CHAPTER FIVE

LEANDER IGNORED ALL Kate's shouts. His mind was made up. He was leaving. He would make some calls from his car and get the hell out of California. Drive somewhere where a storm wasn't raging.

There was a storm enough raging in his guts, self-recriminations flying through his head.

Theós, he'd been on the verge of losing his head completely and kissing her. The ache of desire had infected the whole of him, an internal battle waging to turn around and go straight back to her, sweep her in his arms, carry her to his bed and devour her whole.

His driver opened the door for him and kept a secure hold of it to stop the wind from ripping it off its hinges.

About to climb in, Leander made the fatal error of turning his head.

Kate was quick on her feet. She should already have reached the natural curve the path made and be in sight.

When Kate ran out of English curses, she muttered all the Greek ones Leander had taught her when she hadn't been the anti-Christ to him, and fought the very real need to burst into tears.

This had to count as the worst day of her life, on a par with the day she'd learned that she'd failed the final unit of assessment of her first module at university, bringing her overall mark down and so failing the entire module. Her second-worst fear had come true. Failing the module had terrified her, proved she couldn't take her foot off the gas even for a second. She'd ended her fledging relationship with Euan on the spot and thrown herself even harder into her studies. After resitting the assessment, she'd spent weeks living with cold fear while awaiting the results. A second failure would mean her ultimate worst fear coming true—being kicked out of university and her dreams being destroyed. All the sacrifices she'd made and her family had made would have been for nothing.

This day was as different from failure day as the sun was to the moon but she felt every bit as wretched. She was starving hungry, and physically and emotionally exhausted. It was like Leander had taken possession of her, and not only of her mind. If he'd kissed her, she wouldn't have stopped him. The difference between them would have been that if he'd kissed her, it would have been because she was female and had a pulse. If he'd kissed her she'd have responded because she'd have been helpless to resist.

There was no denying it any more. The thrills that had ravaged her entire being to have his hands cradling her cheeks and his breath on her face… She'd fallen for

Leander. She'd fallen for the man she'd travelled thousands of miles to deliver back to her best friend so he could play the role of her best friend's husband, a man who'd been the light of her existence for five glorious days but had turned on a dime against her, and now she was sat on this stupid pavement in the dark, trees creaking around her in the wind, and with a gashed knee. She didn't know what was the most urgent: stemming her tears or stemming the blood.

The outside sensor lights came back on at the same moment a tall figure emerged on the path and a splash of rain landed on her nose.

Her throat choking, stemming the tears won, and she frantically swallowed the rest back. She would not let him see her cry.

It was only when Leander crouched on his haunches beside her and the humiliation of sitting on a path with a bleeding knee like a small child hit her and smashed into all the other emotions lacing her blood.

'Go away,' she choked, slapping her palm over the wound.

'You're hurt. What's happened?'

'I tripped.' How dare he fake concern? How very *dare* he?

'Let me see.'

'Why? So you can stick your finger in it?' Scrambling to her feet, she hobbled towards the car, raindrops mingling with the blood trickling down her leg. She didn't know what hurt the most, her knee, her toe, her pride or her heart.

She'd fallen for Leander and he despised everything about her. That was what he'd meant. She hadn't done anything to make him hate her except exist.

'Where are you going?'

'Home. You win.' She couldn't do this any more. Not now. Leander would go back to Helena when he was good and ready and not a minute sooner. The only thing Kate would achieve by staying was starvation and, she painfully suspected, hurt of a kind that would leave her with a much bigger wound than a gashed knee. 'You can tell your driver to take me to the airfield.'

She could hear the gritting of his teeth as he called after her through the now pouring rain, 'You need to dress the wound. Come back up and I'll—'

Her anger and pain finally boiled over. Spinning around, she yelled, 'You'll what? Clean it with salt? I'd much rather take my chances with an infection than let you and your hatred anywhere near me, so why don't you just—'

He moved so quickly and stealthily that she didn't notice him close the gap between them until she'd been scooped into his arms.

'You are not flying anywhere in this weather or going anywhere with that wound,' he snarled, already striding back up the path before she found the voice to protest.

'I'm perfectly capable of walking,' she snarled back, kicking her heel hard into his rock-like abdomen.

He gave no reaction whatsoever, opening the gate without loosening his grip on her and then adjusting his arms to secure her more tightly to him as he marched her through the quickly accumulating rainwater deepening on the balcony. The rain now falling like a sheet, the collars of Leander's shirt and jacket were drenched against her sopping cheek.

She wriggled frantically, lashing out with her legs which, with Leander's arm now under her knees and his hand holding her thighs firmly to his chest, meant ineffectually kicking her ankles. 'Put me *down*.'

'You haven't got anything on your feet!' he told her furiously. 'There is debris all over the place from the winds. Do you want to cause more damage to yourself?'

'Like you care!' she spat.

'Of course I bloody care!' he roared, coming to an abrupt stop and tilting his furious face down so his eyes bore into hers. 'You can have *no* idea…' He shook his head and sucked his words away, muttering something that sounded like one of his Greek curses.

He stared into her eyes another long moment and then something tortured contorted his features and, with another curse, his mouth came crashing down on hers in a kiss so hungry and possessive that she froze in shock. At least, her brain froze. The rest of her…

It was like a switch had been turned on. Before she could comprehend what she was doing, she was kissing him back with equal ferocity, melting into the dark heat of his mouth, her hand holding tightly to his neck as their tongues entwined and the fusion deepened. Dimly, she was aware of the rain still falling in a torrent over them, droplets pooling into the tiny pockets their mouths made as they moved together, her fingers now tugging at the sopping hair at the back of his neck, his fingers pressing tightly into her flesh, every passing second bringing them closer to being one entity until only the need for air forced their faces apart.

Blinking rainwater out of her eyes, she stared at him and shook her head in a futile attempt to clear the fog in her mind. It wasn't just the need to draw breath that made it hard to speak but the thrashing of her heart. 'Why did you do that?' she half accused. 'You hate me.'

Leander already knew he was defeated. He'd known it when the scratching of his heart at Kate's failure to round the curve of the path had led him to go and find her. He'd known it when he'd lifted her into his arms. And he'd known it when he'd looked down at her furious face and felt like he would die if he didn't feed the craving for her.

Pressing his forehead to hers, he expelled a long sigh. 'The only thing I hate about you, *agápi mou*, is the way you make me feel.'

Even with the storm raging around them, the silence that followed this admission was so total a feather swooshing to the ground would have been audible.

Jade eyes widened in dazed incomprehension.

A bolt of lightning crackled and lit the sky.

They both looked up and then back at each other. The dazed incomprehension was still vivid.

Wordlessly, he carried her inside and sat her on the sofa she'd made herself at home on. She didn't resist.

She didn't say or do anything but keep her confused eyes fixed on his face.

'I'll get the first aid kit,' he told her as he straightened and ran his fingers through his hair to pull some of the water out.

She blinked as if not understanding. She looked like a drowned rat. A very beautiful drowned rat.

He dropped his gaze to her knee. The wound was still bleeding. All the rain had mingled with it and turned her calf and bare foot red.

Snatching a handful of tissues from the box on the coffee table, he pressed them to her knee. 'Hold that,' he ordered gently. 'I'll be back in a minute.'

She obeyed without uttering a word.

In the large utility off the back of the kitchen, Leander pulled apart the medicine cabinet his staff kept topped up, grabbed the first aid kit, then snatched a couple of fresh towels from the laundry section and headed back to the woman he firmly believed had been put on this earth to make him lose his mind.

Theós, the taste of her mouth on his tongue and the heat and weight of her body in his arms and against his chest were still vivid.

Strangely, he felt calmer now. His heart still throbbed painfully and desire still racked his body but there was relief in not having to hide away from it any more. It was out in the open.

The last time he'd tried to bury his feelings and hide them from the person they most affected had ended in acrimony. When he'd finally admitted the truth fourteen years ago, Leonidas had taken it personally. He'd never forgiven him. But the truth had freed Leander even if the consequence had been to rip a piece of his soul off.

Nothing could come of the freedom that came with Kate knowing the truth. He'd known from the moment desire for her had almost doubled him over that it was a desire that was impossible. Days from marrying their mutual close friend, it had been easier to bear when he'd thought it a one-way desire.

His instincts that her feelings for him had shifted had been proved right. She did want him.

He should have left California when he first felt that shift.

Too late now.

What they felt for each other couldn't go anywhere.

His guts twisted to know he'd never cared if his desire could go anywhere before. Indiscriminate in his affairs, one night of pleasure, one week or one month, it had all been the same to him.

But those women had not been Kate.

Kate held the tissues now soaked in blood to her knee and swallowed hard when Leander reappeared. She was still reeling from the passionate kiss they'd shared and all the feelings that had erupted in her from it, still reeling from what he'd said to her, hardly daring to believe what he'd meant by it, terrified to even contemplate the implications.

He'd taken his jacket off. Her heart clenched to see

smears of her blood on his soaked shirt. Something lower and deeper within her clenched to notice how his shirt had become translucent.

'I'm sorry, I've bled over your rug,' she whispered. She had a vague awareness the rug would have cost far more than she'd received for the battered car she'd sold the day before she'd flown out to Greece.

'It will clean,' he said, handing her a towel. 'For your hair,' he explained before pulling a footrest next to the side of her injured leg and sitting on it. 'Let me take care of your injury.' He gave a fleeting smile. 'No salt, I promise.'

Her heart expanded and caught in her throat. 'Leander…'

'Let me tend to your wound and then we can talk. Okay?'

Trying her hardest to keep herself together, Kate gazed into Leander's steady dark eyes and gave a short nod. Desperately needing to lighten the mood, she said. 'If it gets infected I'll have to sue you. I might sue anyway, seeing as it was your stupid step I lost my footing on.'

Deadpan, he answered, 'I'll give you my lawyer's details, now put your leg on my lap.'

Holding her breath, Kate lifted her leg and laid her calf on his thigh.

'Dry your hair,' he chided as he rummaged through the first aid kit.

She managed a half-smile and patted the towel to her hair. How, she wondered dazedly, was it possible for desire to spring from nothing to everything in the blink of an eye? When Leander shifted the footstool closer to her so more of her thigh lay on his lap, she concentrated harder on holding her breath and prayed he couldn't hear the thundering of her heart.

Oh, what did it matter? He already knew. Her ardent response to his kiss had given her feelings away.

What his own feelings were, she hardly dared to imagine.

Detaching from his mind that it was Kate's leg draped over his thighs and that the texture of her skin was even softer than he'd dreamed, Leander dropped the bloodied tissues stemming the wound on the rug and studied the gash on the base of her knee. It was already clotting, drying blood streaked all down the calf and ankle.

He dabbed at the wound with antiseptic and cleaned the skin around it, working as gently as he could. 'I think this needs butterfly stitches or you'll end up with a nasty scar.'

She gave a half-hearted shrug. 'It doesn't matter. I'm bound to end my career covered in them.'

Removing the backing off a large skin coloured plaster, he distracted himself further from the torture of touching Kate's skin by asking, 'Have you ever been bitten by a patient?'

'Not yet but it's bound to happen one day.'

'Let's hope it's not by one of those other wild creatures you mentioned.'

Although Kate was shortly to join a charity that

cared for orphaned orangutans, the veterinary staff there also treated injured native wild animals as needed. She'd enthusiastically told him all about her upcoming move to South East Asia and what the job would entail at Helena's prompting on her second night, when they'd been eating at a taverna on a neighbouring island. He'd been struck not only by her single-minded focus—Kate had spent her whole life working to reach this point—but by the light in her eyes and the animation in her voice. *Theós*, she'd been fascinating. He could have listened to her talk all night. He could have *watched* her talk all night.

He should have known he was in trouble then.

He wouldn't have known how much damned trouble though.

The memory of Dimitri palming Kate's stomach and leaning his torso into her back to dance with her with that drunken leer on his face smashed back into him. One of his closest friends. A friendship Leander would have killed if he'd acted on the violence of his thoughts.

Coming hot on the heels of being doubled over with desire just from watching her dance, that was the moment he'd known just how much trouble he was in.

'I'm sure you'll be hoping one of them bites my entire head off,' she jested weakly.

It took everything he had to fight the swell of emotions rushing up his throat and spread the plaster over the wound.

She flinched when he pressed his palm down to secure it, only a reflex flinch, barely perceptible, but it broke something in him.

In an instant everything he'd been trying to tune out while tending to her injury, that this was *Kate's* leg draped over him, that this was *her* skin he was touching and it was the smoothest, warmest, silkiest flesh in existence, that the taste on his tongue was the taste of *her* tongue...it all slammed into his senses, and in that instant his senses refilled with her. With Kate.

Heart suddenly pounding furiously, breaths suddenly shallow, Leander lifted his gaze to the beautiful, delicate pixie face with its delicate features and delicate little sticky-out ears. Everything about Kate was delicate, a physicality that couldn't have contrasted more strongly with the vivacious substance contained within it.

Kate only had to walk into a room to light it up.

She only had to fix those incredible jade eyes on him to light *him* up.

Those eyes had lit him up from the very first moment they'd locked onto his, and they were locked on him now.

God help him but he'd hurt her. He'd knocked the light out of her eyes. He'd done that. Deliberately. And now he felt it, the full magnitude of it, as deeply as if he'd inflicted the wounds on himself, but even more than that, he felt the essence of Kate Hawkins feeding into the very fabric of his being.

Kate's heart was thumping so hard she could hardly draw breath. The pain in her knee was entirely forgotten.

The look in Leander's eyes…

It sucked all the air from her lungs.

She'd never seen anything like it before.

The emotion filling them was the antithesis of loathing.

Seeing that emotion…*feeling* it…

Everything fell into place, and suddenly she found herself clutching tightly to the towel and frantically shaking her head. 'We can't,' she choked. '*I* can't.'

'Why the hell do you think I've been trying so hard to make you leave?' he asked hoarsely.

Their gazes held for the longest time before a sharp pain sliced through her chest and she felt her entire being crumple.

This…

Oh, God, this was worse than believing he hated her. This…

With a heavy, sinking stomach, she realised that a part of her had sensed Leander's feelings. Sensed them and ignored them with the same zeal that she'd ignored her own feelings. Refused to even acknowledge their existence.

She'd thought the dreams had been about *her* feelings but they'd been much more than that.

This had been there between them from the start and she hadn't even known it, and now it was too late to wind the clock back to ignorance.

It hit her again. Leander didn't hate her. He had feelings for her.

Fresh hot tears welling, Kate blinked them away. 'Helena is like a sister to me.'

Hating to see the contortion of her face, Leander rubbed the back of his neck. 'She's like a sister to me too. There is nothing else between us.'

'I know, but you're married to her.'

'I'm not.'

Her upset and frustration visibly grew. 'Your brother made his vows and signed the certificate as you.'

'I didn't make those vows and Leo will never allow the certificate to be registered.' This aspect, he was certain, was the most important point to get through to her. He'd seen the two women together, seen their closeness, knew that if Kate believed he was currently married to Helena even on a mere technical level then guilt at their fleeting kiss would eat her up.

'How can you *know* that?'

'Because I know him. He will leave it for me to register.'

She blinked rapidly and then breathed deeply through her nose and slid her leg off his thigh. Throat moving, she straightened, and when she next looked at him, it was beseechingly. 'Leander, you *have* to get the marriage registered, for Helena's sake. You know that.' Her throat moved again. 'And we need to pretend that nothing happened. Just forget about it.'

'That's impossible.' Leander could no more pretend that he'd not had a taste of Kate's sweet lips than he could pretend the earth didn't revolve around the sun.

Her eyes pleaded with him.

'Toothpaste cannot be squeezed back into its tube.'

She spluttered a tearful laugh. 'That is a *terrible* analogy.'

'But a truthful one.'

After the longest time she looked away from him and rubbed her eye with the palm of her hand. Her melodious voice laced with misery, she said, 'I should go.'

'I know. But in this weather…?' Leander shook his head. It felt like a boulder had lodged itself in his chest. His efforts to force Kate from his home had finally worked but it was all too late. He'd treated her despicably for nothing, and he would have to live with it on his conscience for the rest of his life, just as he still lived with his betrayal of his brother. 'Are you hungry?'

Her blonde eyebrows rose in surprise at the question and then quirked as if she couldn't believe he'd been stupid enough to ask it.

'We can't put the toothpaste back in the tube but we can agree not to talk about it,' he said gently. 'I will get my chef to make us something to eat—'

Her eyebrows shot back up again. 'It's the middle of the night.'

'I have staff on call at all times. I think we could both benefit from a shower and dry clothes, and then we can eat and talk about everything except…*this*… until the weather clears enough for you to fly home. What do you say?'

The pulse at the base of his jaw throbbed strongly as he waited for Kate's answer.

The longing crushed Kate's heart against her ribs,

and as she soaked in the face of the man who'd woken up a side of herself she'd barely been aware lived inside her, it hit her again that Leander had feelings for her. Strong feelings.

His toothpaste analogy had been terrible, but it had also been true. They couldn't pretend what had been revealed between them hadn't been revealed, but if they didn't speak about it then it could be squashed away and for a short while they could reset things and maybe even part ways with the spirit of friendship that had first bound them.

She took a deep breath. 'I must really stink if you're offering me the use of your shower.'

A glimmer of amusement passed between them and then Kate found herself laughing while simultaneously wiping a tear away.

CHAPTER SIX

KATE FOLLOWED LEANDER up the dark wood winding staircase and onto a magnificent mezzanine that overlooked a reception room with a marble fountain as its centrepiece.

He unlocked a door and opened it for her. 'My main guestroom. It has its own bathroom. You don't need instructions to work the shower—it is easy to use.'

'What, even for a dumb blonde like me?' she jested again, gripping the first aid kit he'd insisted she bring up with her in case the plaster came off in the shower. She needed to keep things light; anything to stop the tightness in her chest from loosening and for all the emotions she'd packed in it to come spilling out.

He stretched his neck and closed his eyes. 'I am sorry for saying that. I never meant it.'

'I know.'

His stare zoomed back on her. 'Do you?'

She nodded and sighed. 'I knew you were only saying it to get rid of me.'

He studied her a moment and nodded. 'Help yourself to whatever you need. I will find a shirt or something for you to wear.'

'Thank you.'

'I think it's the least I can do after the way I've treated you.'

Seeing him turn as if about to walk away, she impulsively said, 'Leander, when the weather clears and it's safe to fly...*please* go back to Greece. Leo was so angry and he seems to really hate Helena... I'm scared he's going to blow everything up.'

His huge shoulders rose slowly, dark eyes locking back to hers. 'He won't.'

'How can you be so certain?'

'Because he's my twin.'

'You seem so sure of what he'll do but you've barely spoken in years.'

'He's still my twin. I know him better than anyone. He will hate me and curse me but he will keep up the pretence until I return.'

'But what if he's discovered before then?' she challenged softly. 'The press will be itching to get that honeymoon shot of the bride and groom. One photo and everyone will know the wrong brother's on the honeymoon.'

'We are physically identical. No one will be able to tell the difference.'

'I knew it wasn't you the second we walked into the church.'

Her words punched into Leander's chest and sent blood pounding into his head.

Breathing deeply through his nose, he said, 'Our parents struggle to tell the difference between us.'

The first eighteen years of Leander's life had been spent correcting people that they'd addressed the wrong twin. Fourteen years later and any unexpected visit to his family always began with their eyes narrowing to scrutinise which twin was standing before them. His parents always got it right but with his grandparents it went either way. He'd had a girlfriend a few years back, before Leo had cut him off completely, who'd bumped into Leo at a party and spent five minutes talking to him before realising it was the wrong twin, and only then because Leo corrected her. This was a woman Leander had been intimate with. To think that Kate could tell from just one look that it was him...

'Leander, you're identical but you're not the same person,' she said, oblivious to the effect her observation was having on him. 'Your brother holds himself in an entirely different way to you—I knew it was the wrong twin without even seeing his face.'

For the second time in less than a minute it felt like Kate had winded him with her words, and he had to loosen his throat to say, 'Then you will just have to trust me that you are an anomaly on this.'

Leander folded the dark grey shirt and navy sweater over the mezzanine railing opposite the guestroom door, and went straight back into his bedroom to use his own shower.

It took all his mental strength not to let his mind

wander to Kate and the fact that she was, at that moment, likely to be naked, and as he pushed the image of her breasts away, it was replaced with the bewitching smile that had lit her face when he'd caught her kiss in his apartment that night. If she hadn't then turned around and danced over to Helena, she would have seen him almost double over with the strength of the desire that had coursed through him.

That was the moment everything had changed for him.

Even if it hadn't been Kate, the strength of his feelings would have caused him to back away.

Leander was inherently selfish, something his twin had thrown at him too many times over the years to keep count of. Even now, whenever he pictured Leonidas, it was never as the man he was today but as he'd been at eighteen when Leander had told him he was leaving to pursue his life without him, and the hurt and disbelief that had rung from his eyes before cold anger set in. The ramifications from that day still echoed. A combination of living life on his own terms and never wanting to cause such hurt to someone again meant Leander had long ago decided that single life was the life for him. Short-lived flings without any strings or emotional attachments. No mess. No drama. No broken hearts. Perfect.

Pursuing your fake fiancée's maid of honour in the build-up to your sham wedding was low, even for him, and so when he'd met Kate there had been no thoughts of a potential fling. He'd been able to enjoy her company as one human to another, and her company had been fantastic. He'd never had long, intense conversations about absolute rubbish before and then in the next breath long, intense conversations about the world. Once desire had reared its ugly head...

Hours after his desire ignited he'd sat in his Athenian apartment's kitchen listening to the silence only people who'd spent the night over-indulging could make when they finally crashed out, and known he must never be alone with her again.

As Leander had predicted, Kate's plaster came off in the shower. After scrubbing every inch of her body in the most beautifully scented shower cream and washing her hair in equally beautiful shampoo, she wrapped herself in the huge, fluffy towel from the heated rail and put a fresh plaster on. Her skin still sang from when Leander had put the first one on.

She'd never known it was possible for skin to sing at another human's touch.

The song her skin was singing now though, was a lament.

Her throat closed at the impossibility of her longing.

In less than a week she would be flying to Borneo.

She felt like a runner who'd spent their whole life racing a marathon and could finally see the finish line. The marathon had been hard fought, not just by herself but her support crew, namely her parents who'd worked all hours to pay for the tuition needed to help her achieve the scholarship and all the other things they'd done to support her. Then there were her brothers, always so bemused at having a 'swot' for a sister, alternating between teasing and indulgence as the mood took them but always so proud with each marathon mile she passed. And then there was Helena. All the late nights in their dorm room helping Kate revise for school exams, a constant source of emotional support and understanding throughout her university years... All these wonderful people who loved her and were invested in helping Kate realise her dreams.

To do anything to derail that dream's realisation when she could almost touch the finish line was madness, and even if she did think the risk of letting something happen with Leander was worth the potential derailing, it didn't change the fact that very soon he would be flying back to Helena.

Leander was showered and dressed and staring out of the glass wall at the howling wind and lashing rain that kept activating the night sensors when he heard the rustle of movement behind him.

His heart tightened and then expanded like a balloon.

His shirt fitted Kate like an oversized dress. Landing just below her knees, it only enhanced her slenderness. Her dark blonde hair was damp and swung gently over her shoulders. Even with the distance between them he could smell the perfume of her shower and he knew that if he were to close his eyes and inhale deeply he'd be able to breathe in the clean heat of her skin.

He had to work hard to stop his mind fully registering that beneath it, she was likely naked.

For the longest time neither of them spoke.

'How's your knee?'

She held her hands out and pulled her shoulders in. 'I found some butterfly stitches in the kit to use on it. Shame you haven't got any superglue.'

He grinned. Kate's humour had made him laugh from the outset and to hear it now eased a little of the tension that had built back in him since they'd parted for their separate showers. 'Do you need painkillers?'

'It doesn't hurt that badly.' In comparison to the pain in Kate's heart, her knee didn't hurt at all. 'It's almost fully clotted. Can I smell pancakes?'

'Your sense of smell is incredible. Everything's set up in the dining room.'

'Ooh, am I allowed in there now?' she asked with a grin.

Appreciating the effort it must be costing her to make it appear that she didn't have a care in the world, he responded in kind, waving an arm expansively. 'I have unlocked all the doors. Consider yourself free to go where ever you please.'

Kate gave a mock curtsey. 'If I'd known all it would take for you to be nice to me was to cut my knee open, I'd have tripped on the pathway sooner.'

The dining room was as incredible as the main living area, with a glass wall that overlooked the rear—or was it the front?—of the mansion. It being pitch black outside meant any view was a secret waiting to be discovered. She would not allow herself to wish that the night and its accompanying storm lasted long enough for her to see it.

'What time is it?' she asked, taking the seat Leander pulled out for her.

'Just turned three.'

'Is that all?' she marvelled. She was determined to maintain a cheerful front. There had been enough bitterness between them these last two days to last her a lifetime and now she wanted it cleansed. 'I was sure it must be close to sunrise.' She wriggled her chair closer to the table. 'I've definitely lost all sense of time.' Which reminded her, 'I don't suppose you've got a phone charger I can borrow, have you? My battery's dead.'

'Of course. I'll get one brought in for you.'

No sooner had he answered than two members of staff descended with a mound of American pancakes and bacon and a copper *briki* pot of coffee. If they were put out at having to work at this godforsaken time, they didn't show it. Still, Kate reminded herself, they did work for Leander, a man who played as hard as he worked. A man who had every intention of always playing hard.

Although Kate had gone nearly two days without food, her stomach felt so tight that she doubted she'd be able to manage more than one pancake, but a single bite was enough to get her tastebuds going.

'I'm sorry for trying to starve you,' Leander said,

watching with a fist around his heart as she poured maple syrup over a third pancake.

She smiled. 'You would never have beaten me that way.'

He raised an eyebrow. 'And you know that how?'

'I spent five years as a hungry student, remember?'

'Even so, it was cruel of me.' The more he reflected on his behaviour these past two days, the more self-loathing curdled in his guts. Leander knew he was selfish and arrogant but he'd never known he was capable of cruelty. It was a side to himself that sickened him.

'I invaded your home uninvited. You were under no obligation to provide me with anything.' The tiniest sparkle glittered in her eyes. 'The moussaka was a masterstroke.'

He couldn't keep the carefree act up any more. 'No. It was cruel. I wish I could take it back.'

'You were doing what you thought you had to do and...' She shook her head. 'At least now when we say goodbye it will be as the friends we were before.' Her forehead creased and with it her own carefree projection disappeared. 'We were friends, weren't we?'

'We can never go back to that now, Kate.'

'I know... But we *were* friends, weren't we? I didn't imagine it, did I?'

The yearning to reach his hand across the table to her was so strong he fisted it and held it to his stomach. 'No. You didn't imagine it.'

She closed her eyes and inhaled deeply through her nose, then picked her fork back up to stab at her pancake.

After she'd eaten a little more, she looked back at him. 'What you said earlier... I get why you're confident Leo will pretend to be you until you go back, but how do you know he won't register the marriage certificate?'

Leander pushed his plate aside and considered his answer. 'He has always been straight down the line, if you know what I mean. His conscience will not allow a falsely signed document to be registered. He will leave that for me to do.'

Another tiny sparkle glittered. 'Is that because you don't have a conscience?'

He gave a half-smile. 'Because he believes I don't.'

She ate one more bite of her pancake and pushed her own plate aside. 'What happened between you? Helena told me it goes back years but I honestly don't understand how two people formed from the same egg can be estranged as you two are.'

He poured himself another coffee and topped Kate's up too, remembering her first breakfast on his island when he'd poured her a cup of it. The face she'd pulled at the taste had amused him and made Helena snort with laughter. Greek coffee was, he'd learned in his thirty-two years on this earth, an acquired taste. Four breakfasts later and Kate had drunk it like a native.

'Before I answer that, answer something for me.' It was a question that kept repeating itself in his mind because of the sheer impossibility of it. 'Could you really tell it was Leo waiting at the altar and not me?'

Her eyes widened in disbelief. 'Could *I* tell? Honestly, I couldn't believe no one else noticed. I watched them exchange their vows fully expecting someone to jump up and point out the wrong brother was standing there. It was the most surreal experience of my life but no one else noticed. I'm pretty sure even your parents didn't clock that it was Leo until the vows were done.'

'But you saw it?' Leander pressed.

'I didn't even think about it.' Her slender shoulders rose and she added a simple, 'It wasn't you.'

For a moment it felt like he'd fallen into a version of suspended animation where the only sound was the blood pounding in his ears.

Clearing his throat, he said, 'People have never been able to tell us apart. They think we are the same person.'

The face she pulled at this made him smile properly for the first time in days.

'We are physically identical but our personalities have always been very different,' he confirmed drily. 'Leo was always very serious, very straight down the line, as I said.' Still staring intently at her, he took a sip of his coffee. 'You know why I have never wanted to marry or be tied down with a partner?'

Her pretty dark blonde eyebrows drew together.

'It's because I spent eighteen years married to my brother and our marriage ended with acrimony. I hurt him very badly.' For reasons he couldn't begin to decipher, it felt imperative that he explain himself, something he'd never needed to do before. 'People treated us as if we were one entity with the same thoughts and opinions. It frustrated both of us, especially in our teenage years. Leo frustrated me. He still does. He is so straight, never willing to take risks. He was always the voice of reason.'

'He was your conscience?'

'In a way, yes. He shackled me but his opinion mattered more to me than anyone's.' He shook his head with a grimace. 'It's complicated.'

'It sounds it,' she said softly.

'We were close growing up.' It had only been since hearing Leo's voice that he'd remembered just how close they'd been. All the fun they'd had. How they could hold conversations without even having to speak. 'We knew for a long time that when we turned eighteen and finished school, we could either join the family business and work our way through the ranks until we gained the experience needed to take over, or we could take a cash sum from our parents and make our own way in the world. Leo stayed and I took the cash.'

'And that caused the estrangement?'

'It's what started it.'

'Because you chose to go?'

'Because I'd let him believe I would stay.'

Understanding flared. 'Ah.'

The muscles of his neck tightening as he related for the first time the day he'd put a knife to all their plans, Leander kneaded at them. 'I told him I was taking the cash the day we finished our education. A week later I left home to make my own way in the world.'

'He felt that you'd abandoned him?' she guessed.

He grimaced, gut curdling with more self-loathing. 'Yes. I fed us both all the excuses in the world but that is what it came down to. I love my brother, he's a part of me, but at the time I just wanted to be Leander first rather than one of the Liassidis twins, and recognised in my own right. I wanted to make my own way, to get out there and *see* the world. I should have been honest from the start but I got caught up in all his plans for our future with Liassidis Shipping and only found the courage to tell him after I'd booked my flight to America.' He kneaded harder at his neck. 'Leo was furious.' He gazed into the jade eyes bruised with lack of sleep and admitted for the first time, 'And hurt. It would have been better if I had given him the knife to stab into his own back.' And stab himself too.

Hurting Leonidas had felt like cutting his own artery. Leander would never change the path he'd taken but if he could go back and find the courage to tell Leo sooner so he could prepare himself for the separation, he would do it in a heartbeat.

She winced but didn't say anything.

'But we are identical twins. The bond between us can never be fully broken and for many years we both made the effort to get past my betrayal—and it was a betrayal—and then all the crap happened with the business... Do you know about that? When Liassidis Shipping came close to going under?'

'Helena told me a little about it,' Kate said, thinking hard through the exhaustion creeping through her veins that zero sleep and a full stomach had set off.

She knew Helena's parents had been business partners of a sort—the details were currently hazy in her mind—with Leander and Leo's parents, and that after Helena's father died her mother had done something or other with her share that had put the business in jeopardy. 'But it was all resolved, wasn't it?'

'It was resolved and the business is thriving now,' he agreed, 'but Leo has never forgiven me for not going home and helping to resolve it, and until I called him Saturday morning we hadn't seen or spoken to each other in five years.'

Although Kate knew the Liassidis twins were estranged, this was the first time she'd really contemplated what the estrangement meant. Her brothers infuriated her at times—and she no doubt infuriated them—and she'd seen little of them during her university years, but she couldn't imagine cutting them out of her life altogether.

She smothered a yawn and finished her coffee, hoping another shot of caffeine would help fight the encroaching sleepiness. This was all the time she would ever have left with Leander and she didn't want a second of it lost in the fog of exhaustion. 'Don't you miss him?'

His jaw tightened, a pulse throbbing below his ear. 'In the years after I left home we only saw each other sporadically. We were already accustomed to our lives being separate.'

Not a direct answer, she noted, her heart twisting for him being unable to admit what to Kate was obvious. Instead of pressing it, she tried another tack. 'Why didn't you go home when the business was in trouble?'

'Because he didn't want me there.'

'But you just said he hasn't forgiven you for not being there,' she pointed out, confused.

'He told me that he didn't want me there and that he would deal with it. I took him at his word—his brain is laser sharp. He can solve a problem before anyone else has identified that there even is a problem. My field is technology, not shipping. I had nothing practical to offer apart from my cash and he made it very clear that he didn't want that either.'

She smothered another yawn and blinked hard to refresh her gritty eyes. 'Do you think he was hoping you'd ignore his order to stay away and go home anyway?'

'Whatever I did, I was damned in his eyes. I think he was waiting for the excuse to justify to himself severing the final ties between us. Up to then, it had been me who'd made all the effort to keep our relationship going but after that he stopped answering my calls or responding to my messages.'

'Maybe it was support of an emotional kind he wanted from you, the kind that you don't always know you need until you receive it or miss until you don't get it,' she suggested, thinking of all the times she'd been too frazzled with exams to call her parents and let them know she was alive and them turning up at her digs with bags of food that required no greater preparation than sticking in the microwave. They'd understood what she needed in those times better than she had.

Leander gave a guttural laugh. 'Emotional support? I thought you'd met my brother.'

'He's like an ice box but he's still human,' she said quietly. She felt wretched for both brothers. She'd always been prepared to dislike Leo after the way Helena had spoken about him but now she felt a huge pang of sympathy for both men, one too stubborn to tell his brother that he needed him, the other too stubborn to see his brother needed him.

A yawn sneaked up on her which she couldn't suppress and which she only just managed to cover with the back of her hand. She blinked hard again at the gritty tiredness in her eyes. 'Excuse me.'

The dark eyes that had barely left her face the entire conversation softened. 'You're exhausted.'

She tried to inject some lightness back. 'Well, it's almost morning and I didn't get much sleep last night.'

His wince of self-recrimination showed her attempted lightness hadn't landed. 'I'm sorry for what I put you through. A thousand times sorry. It was unforgivable of me.'

'It's already forgiven.'

He held her stare for the longest time before exhaling. 'That's more than I deserve.'

'Stop it. You did what you had to do. If I'd understood my own feelings sooner then—' She cut herself off before she could say words that could never be taken back, and gave a frustrated, helpless shrug. 'Toothpaste.'

He shook his head. 'If it's any consolation, I hardly slept either.' Then he added with a short laugh, 'Toothpaste.'

Her own short laugh was interrupted by a wide yawn she only just managed to raise her hand to cover.

Leander didn't know if it was the exhaustion etched on Kate's face that did it or the valiant way she was trying to fight it, but his heart turned over. 'You should sleep.'

She shook her head vehemently. 'I'll sleep on the plane...' Another enormous yawn overcame her.

Before he could stop to think, he pushed his chair back and got to his feet. 'You need sleep, Kate. It might be hours until it's safe to fly. Get some proper sleep in a proper bed, if not for your sake then for mine—let me absolve some of my guilt.'

CHAPTER SEVEN

LEGS FEELING LIKE dead weights beneath her, knee throbbing, the toe she'd hurt throbbing too, Kate followed Leander up the winding stairs and onto the dimly illuminated mezzanine.

It was still black outside but the night would soon be over. When she woke, the dying storm would be over too and with it her time with Leander. The dejection she felt at this...

He opened the door of the pretty, neutrally decorated guestroom she'd showered in and stepped aside. 'If you need anything in the night, food or drink, just dial—'

'One on the intercom?'

His smile was as bleak as the dejection in her heart.

'Can I ask you something?' she asked before he could make the move that would finally separate them that night. As exhausted as she was, she wasn't ready to say goodnight to him. Not ready for oblivion. Not when to wake from oblivion would likely mean saying goodbye to Leander for ever.

'You can ask me anything.'

'Why were you so cold with me after your party?'

This was the one question she needed answered before she left.

'Because I wanted to throw Dimitri out of a window for dancing with you.' Leander swallowed the bile that had risen at the gross overreaction of his thoughts that night. 'Once I went to bed, I tortured myself for the rest of the night that the two of you were in a room alone together. I was…' Realising he was about to say something forbidden, he cut himself off. 'Toothpaste.'

The understanding that flashed in her eyes told him she understood what he'd stopped himself from saying. That he'd been jealous. That it had been the night his desire for Kate had smacked him as hard in the face as he'd wished to smack Dimitri.

'Not my finest hour,' he admitted wryly.

He'd never been jealous before. Like his cruelty towards Kate, it was a side to himself he would never allow to take control of him again.

'Nothing happened between us,' she said softly, and she looked so beautiful and so damned ravishing standing in the doorway with only his shirt wrapped around her naked flesh and the guest bed mere feet behind her that the desire he'd controlled to a simmer while they'd been eating slammed back into him.

'I wouldn't think less of you if it had.' He gave a low laugh. It was time to back away and remove himself from the breathing temptation that was Kate. 'We both know I am in no position to judge.' With a bow of his head, he stepped to his own room and was about to open the door when she called his name.

He turned back to her.

She hadn't moved from the threshold of the guest door. 'I haven't slept with anyone.'

It was like she'd thrown a bucket of ice over him. 'What? Never?'

Beautiful jade eyes locked on his. 'Never.'

Mind completely blown, he walked slowly back to her. 'Why not?'

Her lips curved into a tremulous smile and she rested her cheek on the doorframe. 'Do you remember me telling you about that orangutan documentary I watched with my mum when I was seven?'

He remembered everything she'd ever told him. 'The one that made you announce you wanted to be a vet?'

She nodded. 'Everyone kept telling me that only the really clever kids could be vets. I'm not naturally clever like you, Leander. I was the youngest in my class which put me at a disadvantage when I was little and made me feel stupid. I had to work twice as hard as the other kids just to learn my words and numbers, and that's basically been the story of my life ever since, and always with goals that needed to be reached: working for the scholarship, working for my GCSEs, working for my A-levels and then five years spent working for my degree.'

'I understand all that but Helena has always spoken about all the fun the two of you got up to over the years.'

Her smile was rueful. 'I never said I lived as a nun but I went to an all-girls boarding school. The opportunities to go out and live it up were so limited that they didn't really impact my study schedule. Once I started at university I thought I could cut loose a bit more and I got together with this nice lad studying physics, but seeing Euan made me take my eye off the ball and I stopped studying as hard and came close to failing a module and losing my whole place on the course. It scared the life out of me and I ended things with Euan way before we'd reached the getting our clothes off stage.' Eyes shining, her chin wobbled. 'Back then I assumed it would happen once all my studies were over and the time was right.'

Fighting to control the emotions smashing through him, fighting to breathe, Leander backed himself against the mezzanine.

'What are you thinking?' she whispered in a small voice.

He smothered a groan and rubbed the back of his neck. 'I'm thinking I wish you hadn't told me.'

Her silent hurt at this sliced through him.

'Kate...' This groan refused to remain smothered. 'You do know this means I am now destined to spend my life wondering if it has happened?'

Her attempt at laughter sounded like a sob. 'I can message you when it happens to stop you wondering if you like?'

His own effort at laughter was a failure. 'I don't know if the confirmation would drive me more insane.'

Their gazes stayed locked for the longest time before their chests rose in unison.

'Get some sleep, *agápi mou.*'

Her chest rose again at his endearment, a sad smile curving her pretty little mouth as she backed into her room. 'Goodnight, Leander.'

The door closed softly behind her.

Kate hadn't thought it possible that she'd fall asleep. Her talk with Leander had wiped away her exhaustion. Or so she'd thought. Moments after her head hit the pillow she fell into vivid dreams that all revolved around him, and woke with a sob in her throat, an ache in her heart and a heavy pulse throbbing between her legs. She could still feel the imprint of his mouth on hers.

She cuddled tightly into her pillow.

A tear crept out.

The feelings she had for Leander were all wrong. She was only here to take him back to Helena, and...

And Helena didn't want him.

Not in the way Kate wanted him.

Helena was marrying Leander out of desperation. As soon as the sham honeymoon was over, she'd set the ball rolling to get her inheritance and as soon as she had it, the sham marriage would be over.

Helena loved Leander as a brother, and Kate's heart panged sharply as she recalled a long-forgotten conversation from a few years ago. Leander had been due to visit London and Helena had, as she often did, invited Kate to join them. She'd been studying frantically for her final exams and had needed a break and so had, for once, agreed, only to get herself into a lather at the last minute and beg off, terrified that the time she'd have to spend eating with the two of them would be the difference between pass and failure. Helena, used to Kate's last-minute exam time panics, had laughed. 'One day, I *will* get the two of you in a room together,' she'd said. 'If any man's going to make you want to throw away your chastity belt it's Leander.'

'I thought you said he was a playboy,' Kate had said, confused that Helena was seemingly trying to play cupid.

'He's a playboy but he's a good guy, and seeing as he won't settle down until he's at least fifty and you're planning to marry an orangutan, does him being a play-boy even matter?'

Her heart beating harder than ever, Kate replayed that forgotten conversation again, forgotten because she'd sat her exams soon after and then she'd left uni-versity for good and resumed her volunteer role with the vet team at the zoo twenty miles from her family home, a role she'd undertaken every term break since her second year at uni. Her head had been too full praying not to have failed her degree to even think of Helena's cupid game, and then once it was confirmed that everything she'd worked so hard for had paid off and she'd become a permanent, paid member of the veterinary team, she didn't give Leander Liassidis an-other thought. She didn't give any man a thought, by now too intent on getting the experience she needed to take the final step of realising her dreams. When Helena had confided about her marriage to Leander and the reasons for it, Kate had been in the process of arranging visas and the vaccinations needed for her imminent move to Borneo, too excited that her dream was almost close enough to touch to remember Helena had once implied Leander was the man Kate should lose her virginity to.

This time next week, she would be in South East Asia, finally realising her lifelong dream. All the sacrifices Kate and those she loved had made had paid off. Nothing could derail her from achieving it because it was already done. She'd already reached the finish line.

And now Leander had invaded her dreams. He'd taken them over so effectively that it was like he'd always lived in them, and her heart beat even harder at the realisation that what she was feeling now was so strong that it was impossible to imagine that anyone else could ever make her feel a fraction of what Leander did.

Feeling like she was falling into another one of her Leander dreams, she threw the duvet off and, her heart thrumming, padded to the door.

The sun was starting to rise and still Leander's brain would not switch off.

He'd brushed his teeth to within an inch of their lives but still all he could taste was Kate. He could still feel the heat of her body in his arms. Could still feel the smoothness of her flesh beneath his fingers.

He closed his eyes and fought harder than he'd ever fought for control of himself.

What madness had let him believe he could sleep with Kate only two rooms away from him?

The worst part was knowing that two rooms away, Kate was trapped in her own tortured awareness of him lying here.

Theós, he wanted her so badly. So badly. More than he'd ever wanted anyone or anything.

And she wanted him too...

The tap on his door was so light he thought his febrile mind had conjured it. It was only the surge of his pulses that made him climb out of bed a few moments later and open his door.

Kate was standing with her back against the mezzanine, facing him.

He swallowed, hardly able to breathe. 'Is everything okay?'

'I...' Her voice dropped so low he could hardly hear it. 'I don't want it to be with anyone else.'

His grip on the door tightened and he had to clear his throat to hoarsely speak. 'What are you saying?'

Her voice might be barely audible but there was no mistaking the clarity in her eyes. 'I want it to be with you.'

Another of those silences where a falling feather could be heard enveloped them until, with a groan that rose from the pit of his stomach, he took the three paces needed to scoop her into his arms and any remaining fight in him evaporated.

What was he even fighting for? he wondered dimly as he carried her into his bedroom, soaking in the colour heightened cheeks and all the delicate pixie features that made Kate so unutterably beautiful.

He laid her on his bed. The beats of his thundering heart echoed through the entirety of his body.

A trembling hand pressed into his cheek. The warmth of her touch scorched him. Slowly, her fingers tiptoed to cup the back of his head. Her throat moved numerous times before her chest rose. Her lips parted, shallow breaths escaping and she slowly craned her face to him.

God in heaven, he ached to be a part of her.

Dipping his head, the last thing he saw before their mouths locked together was the melting of the jade into liquid.

The first brush of her lips against his melted *him* into liquid.

Kate's heart was racing so hard and so fast she could no longer feel the individual beats. Everything—*everything*—had become Leander, and she scraped her fingers through his soft hair to knead his skull as the tender caress of his mouth deepened, her nerve endings zinged into life and the entirety of her senses were filled by his dark taste and musky scent.

She couldn't stop this even if she wanted to, and she didn't want to. She wanted this, wanted Leander with every fibre of her being. Nothing else mattered. Nothing in the world but this. Him. Her. Them.

Who else could she give the whole of herself to? Who else could make her feel like this?

She wanted it all. Needed it all.

When he lifted his face to stare back into her eyes, the hooded desire she found contained in the dark depths made her heart catch.

'Leander, I...' She only just caught herself from saying words that could never ever be taken back.

His gaze flickered, lips tightening as if he too were having to stop himself from speaking. Seeing the mirrored torture only made her heart crash to a stop all over again.

Bringing her face back up to his, she stroked her soft cheek against his stubbly cheek and whispered, 'Make love to me. Please, Leander, make love to me.'

His breaths were ragged and heavy in her ear. 'You have no idea what you do to me,' he muttered hoarsely before his hungry mouth recaptured hers and sent flames burning through her.

Her core and heart on fire, Kate closed her eyes and sank into the pleasure of Leander's assault of her senses.

Sensuous lips brushed the swan of her neck, stubble scratching her sensitised skin as he slowly kissed his way down to the top button of her—his—shirt.

Loath though he was to tear an inch of his flesh away from her, Leander dragged himself to his knees and gazed down at the woman who'd become the only woman in existence for him. Never had he seen such open passion in the eyes of a lover. Never had the heat of a touch turned his body into liquid.

But it wasn't just the unadulterated desire radiating at him that made his heart feel so weighty. The trust radiating from Kate's beautiful eyes landed with equal weight.

This gift she was bestowing on him…

Hooking his thumbs in the sides of his boxers, he pulled them down past his hips, lifted his knees to skim them down his legs and chucked them aside with no further thought.

She opened her arms for him.

Painfully aware of how close he already was to the edge, Leander swooped to recapture her mouth.

Kate dissolved into the dark taste of Leander's hard hungry kiss and then the whole of her dissolved into a fever of sensation as he stripped the shirt from her.

Working from the top, button by button was undone, his lips trailing kisses over every millimetre of exposed flesh all the way down to her pubic bone where the shirt had ruched around her waist.

He pulled it apart.

Fully naked beneath a male gaze for the first time in her life, Kate's throat caught tightly at the expression on Leander's face. He was gazing at her like he'd unwrapped a personal gift from the heavens.

How could she have mistaken that look for disgust? she wondered in dim amazement, then stopped wondering about anything when he covered her breast and the sensations that careered through her felt like their own gift from the heavens. When he replaced his hand with his mouth, head spinning, blood on fire, Kate became fully lost in Leander's worshipful touch.

Hands and mouth roamed her body, kissing, stroking, licking, biting, kneading, the delicious scratching of his stubble against her skin only intensifying the pleasure.

So lost in the sensations had she become that when he gently spread her thighs and rested his face in between, it felt like the most necessary and natural act in the world.

She wasn't his gift from the heavens, she thought hazily as she writhed into him. He was her gift, and the more he gave the more she wanted. Her hunger for him was limitless. Every inch of her body was aflame, burning for more of his kisses, more of his touches and when their mouths fused back together and he put his hand where his tongue had just been, she kissed him deeply and arched into him, incapable of doing anything but obeying her body's demands. All of its demands were for Leander. Just him.

Leander was hanging on by a thread. The need to take full possession of Kate had become an agonised fever in his blood, his arousal tipping into unendurable, but through it all, words repeating over and over to keep his passion leashed, *she's a virgin.*

He could scarcely believe how much it felt like his first time too, as if her succulent breasts were the first breasts he'd ever caressed… *Theós*, her body could have been created especially for him, her scent, taste and texture aphrodisiacs designed purely for his own chemical makeup to respond to, everything about her so much more than he'd ever imagined possible.

'*Theós*, Kate, you're so beautiful,' he groaned into her mouth. 'I want you so much.'

Her mouth slanted against his with such passion it spoke louder than any words could that everything he was feeling was shared.

It took the last remaining fragment of his sanity to murmur, 'Let me get protection.'

Her hold around him tightened, her eyes begging him not to let go of her. 'I'm protected.'

Swallowing hard, trying to control the beats of his heart, he clasped her hip, fingers sinking into her bottom, then shifted himself so his erection pressed between her legs. Just knowing he was so close to being where he so desperately needed to be made his arousal throb hard enough to pulse blood to his head.

This was it. The point of no return.

Threading his fingers through hers, Leander captured Kate's mouth for another heady taste of paradise and slowly pushed into her tight velvet heat.

The shock of Leander's huge arousal pressing into her was matched only by the thrills fluttering through her entire body.

It felt like she'd waited her whole life for this moment.

With one of his hands holding hers, the other gripping her hip, the security of his touch would have doused any fear. But she had no fear, not with Leander, and she submitted her body, soul and trust in their entirety to him.

Lips brushing like feathers, he inched inside her, setting off nerve endings buried so deeply inside her she'd never known they were there waiting for his touch to awaken them from dormancy until, finally, their groins were fused as one.

For a long moment they stayed locked like that, Kate gazing with wonder into dark eyes filled with equal wonder until he groaned her name and kissed her tenderly, withdrawing to the tip.

With a half-stifled groan, he filled her again, withdrew, filled her, his movements intense but unhurried, giving her all the time she needed to become accustomed to his possession.

Slowly, the tempo increased. Slowly, Kate felt the core of herself unfurl and bloom as the pleasure of his possession intensified. So slowly did they go that when she instinctively raised her thighs and the friction increased where she most needed it, she was unprepared for her climax, one moment luxuriating in the bliss of being made love to by Leander, the next caught in a rollercoaster of pulsations that had her clinging tightly to him and crying out his name as the rollercoaster shot her to the stars.

Never in his life had Leander witnessed anything as beautiful as the widening of Kate's eyes as she thickened around him and pulled him deeper into her tightness. Her cries of his name echoed dimly in ears that were drowning in the roar of blood as he fused himself as tightly to her as it was possible for two humans to be and cried out at the almost violent pleasure of his own desperately needed release.

* * *

Kate had never believed that time really could stand still, but in those seconds or minutes or hours of silence, broken only by the pounding of her heart in her ears that followed their lovemaking, she finally understood what it meant. Time had ceased to have any meaning. There was no meaning left in the world. Only Leander.

She had never imagined it could be like that, that it wouldn't be just her body that she gave to him but the whole of herself. And that he'd given the whole of himself to her too.

It had been so beautiful.

He'd made her feel beautiful.

Whatever happened when time reset itself, this was a night she would keep close to her heart and cherish for the rest of her life.

Leander could have stayed wrapped in Kate's arms, the beats of their hearts smashing together, breathing in the sweet scent of her hair and cheek for eternity. Only the fear of his weight suffocating her gave him the impetus to move. Even then, he could only bring himself to shift slowly, clasping her hand to pull her with him so she rolled into him.

Nuzzling his mouth and chin into the top of her head, he stroked her back, marvelling anew at the soft silkiness of her skin, marvelling too at how damn pleasurable Kate's delicate fingers making tiny circles over his chest was.

There was no need for words. No need to rehash what had just taken place.

He could barely comprehend how incredible it had been.

'When is your flight to Borneo?' he murmured after the longest, most peaceful time he thought he'd ever spent had passed.

She lifted her face to meet his stare. 'Monday evening.'

He kissed her gently. 'Then stay. Stay with me until Sunday.'

Her jade eyes swirled starkly. 'And then you'll go back to Greece?' she whispered.

'I gave my word,' he said heavily, the weight in his stomach at the thought of returning to his homeland pulling at his vocal cords. Pulling at all of him.

Tears filled her eyes. 'Then give *me* your word that if I stay, you'll go back to Greece on Sunday. You and me… It can't go anywhere. I'm starting a new life thousands of miles away and your place is with…'

To Kate's horror, she couldn't say Helena's name, and suddenly it hit her, the depth of her betrayal of her best friend.

Concern flickered in Leander's stare and then he must have read her thoughts for in seconds he'd rolled her onto her back.

'Listen to me, Kate,' he said, staring intently into her eyes. 'You have done nothing wrong. Helena feels nothing for me. You know that.'

'I know, but—'

'There is no but,' he told her firmly. 'You and I are both free, consenting adults. If she knew about us she'd be pleased, you know that.'

She blinked frantically before taking a deep breath. When she'd gathered herself together, she forced firmness to her own voice. 'You have to be her husband.'

His jaw clenched then loosened. 'I know. And I will. When you fly back to England to pack for your new life, I will return to Greece.'

It hurt more than she could have believed to say, 'You promise?'

'I swear.' Leander kissed the tip of her nose. 'We will go back to the real world on Sunday.' Whatever it cost him. 'But until then, let this time be for us. Just us. Let us pretend the real world doesn't exist.'

She inhaled slowly before the tiniest smile played on the corners of her little pixie mouth. 'I thought it was impossible for you to pretend.'

He kissed her again, harder, arousal stirring back to life. 'For you, my little pixie, I will pretend anything.'

CHAPTER EIGHT

'WHERE ARE WE GOING?' Kate asked as she climbed into the leather passenger seat of the small sports car. She had no idea how Leander had been able to fit his body into the driver's side. She supposed it helped that the roof had already been folded back. She didn't know why he bothered opening the door—his legs were so long he could have just stepped over it.

After two days spent barely surfacing from his bed, Leander had announced as their breakfast was being cleared away from the balcony of his bedroom that he was taking her out.

'Shopping,' he now told her.

'That's the big surprise? Shopping?'

'You don't look impressed.'

'Well, you did big up the surprise aspect.'

He grinned and leaned over for a kiss. 'I assumed you were bored with my wardrobe—you seem reluctant to wear any of it.'

Heat flushing through her, she gave a knowing smile and lifted her feet onto the dashboard, deliberately letting the black shirt of his that she was wearing fall to her thighs.

'Behave,' he growled, putting the car in gear.

'You're the one who insisted we go out. I was happy mooching around your house…'

'Mooching?'

'You can work it out.' She opened a button on her shirt—and it was her shirt. Kate had determined to take every one of the shirts she'd borrowed since her arrival in California with her as mementoes—and exposed her naked breasts. 'Is it me or is it hot here?'

Two days of near constant lovemaking had completely opened Kate's eyes to pleasure. If Leander was a willing teacher in the art of sensuality then she was a very enthusiastic, committed student. Who wanted to waste time browsing through shops when they could be in bed? There was little enough time left as it was…

He kept his gaze on the road in front of him. 'If you are trying to distract me, it's not going to work. I am taking you shopping, Kate, whether you like it or not.'

'I thought billionaires brought the shops to them,' she sulked.

'I'm not buying for me, I'm buying for you, and there isn't time to have you fitted and clothes made bespoke for you, not without employing an army to work around the clock on you, which will take up even more of our valuable time than going into Marina Sands and buying off the peg.'

She sighed and closed the shirt back up. 'Leander, that's very generous of you but I don't need any clothes.'

He turned off his private driveway and onto the main road, changed gear and put his hand on her thigh. 'Believe me, I prefer it when you don't wear *any* clothes.'

She pushed his hand away and primly said, 'Behave.'

Laughing, he captured her hand and brought it to his mouth so he could kiss her fingers. 'I'm taking you out tomorrow night and as sexy as you look in my shirts, you will feel uncomfortable wearing one where we're going.'

Her happy mood dimmed. 'I don't want to go out.'

'Trust me, you'll want to go where I'm taking you.'

'But it's…' She couldn't say it. Couldn't say that it would be their last night together. To vocalise it would make it real. Instead, she said, 'What if you're recognised? You're supposed to be on your honeymoon.'

It was the first time either of them had mentioned the elephant in the room since she'd agreed to stay. There had been no talk about either of their immediate futures at all. Kate's only communication with Helena had been a message she'd sent soon after Leander had made love to her a second time, in which she'd been able to tell her friend truthfully that Leander had promised to return to Greece on Sunday. She'd received some praying emojis in return. Her only other communication had been to her mother, apologising that she wouldn't be home until Sunday. That this would give Kate barely twenty-four hours with her family before her flight to Borneo was something she couldn't bring herself to think about because since then it had been just her and Leander cocooned away from the real world, making love and just…*being*.

They had been the best days of her life and now, leaving the sanctuary of his home only brought home how fleeting the time they had together actually was.

'Kate…' It was his turn to sigh. 'We're safe here, I promise. The only local people I've become friendly with are surfers. No one here follows European tabloids. I'm just another rich guy.'

Accepting defeat, Kate closed her eyes and enjoyed the sensation of the breeze on her face. If they couldn't be in bed together then just being with him was a perfect second best.

'How did you get so rich?' she asked idly as they rounded a sweeping bend. 'Did you have lessons on it at school?'

He laughed. 'Lots of components. Luck and timing played a big part.'

'My dad always says people create their own luck.'

'Your father makes a valid point. I've always had an aptitude for technology and I knew it was the most likely route for me to earn my fortune. When I launched the instant payment app there were three other similar apps in development that I knew of,' Leander explained of the first app he'd created and developed. Its launch had launched his career and founded his wealth. 'My product was better and the security aspect unsurpassable, but if I had made one wrong move or my rivals a better move I would have had to return home.'

'It was all or nothing for you?'

'I invested the entirety of the lump sum my parents gave me in it.'

'So if it had failed you'd have lost everything?'

'It made it easier to take the risk, knowing I had my family to fall back on.'

'Would they have let you join the business seeing as you'd already walked away from it?'

'I wouldn't have joined the business. Shipping bores me. I'd have moved back into my childhood bedroom and found the money to open my own cocktail bar.'

Expecting her to laugh as most people did when he revealed his adolescent fantasy, a warmth filled his chest when she musingly said, 'I can imagine you doing that.'

He pulled a face. 'For real?'

'You make excellent cocktails and you're so out-going and gregarious that people would flock to your bar.' He could feel her eyes on him. 'To be honest, I think it would suit you better than being a tech gazillionaire, and as you now are a gazillionaire, aren't you ever tempted to just sell up and buy yourself that cocktail bar?'

'I have wild moments when I fantasise about it,' he admitted, turning into the main Marina Sands car park.

'What's stopped you? Surely you've proved everything you need to prove?'

He reversed into an empty bay. 'I've never been out to prove anything.'

'If you didn't have something to prove you'd have used your parents' money to open the cocktail bar and become one of those people who doodle their clever ideas on napkins in quiet times with reggae music in the background rather than make their clever ideas a reality.'

He turned the engine off. 'There's no money in cocktail bars. That's why I went into technology.'

She unbuckled her seatbelt and leaned her face into his. 'That's my point, Mr Gazillionaire. You're rich enough to live thousands of lives without running out of money. Retire. Open your cocktail bar. Doodle your clever ideas on napkins...' Her eyes glittered. 'Unless I'm right and you really are still set on proving that your decision to go your own way was the right choice.'

Astounded at her wild observation, Leander responded to the kiss Kate planted on his mouth automatically.

'Let's get this over with,' she declared before flinging her door open.

She'd skipped round to his side of the car before he'd closed the door.

Shades on, hands tightly clasped, they made the short walk to the boulevard, their footsteps leaving indentations in the fine layer of sand covering all the roads and pathways. The breeze would wipe the indentations away by the time they returned to the car, he thought with a stab in his chest. Everything about him and Kate was impermanent, and he strongly suspected that it was the impermanency that made everything between them feel so intense and allowed him to fully commit the whole of himself to what they were sharing. Saying goodbye to Kate would be hard, he did not doubt it, but life was hard and he'd have the sweetest memories to remember her by. No regrets.

What they were sharing was perfect and their ending would be perfect too.

He could not bring himself to contemplate what came after they'd said goodbye.

They'd reached the wide tree-lined boulevard.

Kate's eyes widened in amazement at the array of shops and cafés and the richly dressed people, many of them carrying or walking tiny dogs of a host of varieties, wandering in and out of them. 'Is everyone who lives here rich?'

'Not everyone. The surfers I'm friendly with share a one storey home on the beachfront that was inherited from Danny's grandmother. They work the local bars and restaurants to pay their bills and spend the rest of their lives in the ocean.'

'Was it the surfing that made you buy a property here?' she asked as Leander stopped to check out the name of a boutique, remembering his complete mastery of the board he'd surfed the enormous waves on.

'The surf and Marina Sands being only a short helicopter ride to San Francisco. I usually surf every day when I'm here.'

She adopted an innocent expression. 'Then why has your wetsuit stayed dry these last few days?'

He caught her off-guard by hooking an arm around her waist and burying his face in her hair to whisper,

'Because the competition between catching the surf or staying in bed with you is no competition at all.'

'Then stop wasting time here and take me back to bed,' she whispered back, gripping his hip and pressing herself into him. For the first time since they'd become lovers she was in the frustrating position of having to wait to act on her desires. And she wanted him all the time. Probably it was the strict time limit on what they had together at play, combined with her body making up for twenty-five—nearly twenty-six—years of chastity, together with the fact that Leander was a walking hunk of testosterone. She just could not believe how she'd spent that week in Greece with him, oblivious to how ruddy sexy he was...or wilfully ignoring it as she now accepted she'd done. The more they made love, the more she wanted to make love, her desire for him an ever-expanding hunger that could only be satisfied for short periods of time.

He growled quietly into her ear then brushed a kiss over her mouth. 'Choose a dress and anything else you want and then we can go home. This is the shop I wanted to bring you to.'

In moments Kate was plunged into the alien world of what looked to her inexperienced eyes to be bohemian haute couture. She was quite sure she would normally be in raptures to be brought into a shop like this and told to choose anything she wanted, but right then she was having trouble keeping herself upright. The worst bit was the gleam in Leander's eyes that told her he knew exactly the state he'd put her in.

The shop manager came to them. Leander gave his instructions—let Kate have anything she wanted—and then excused himself.

'Where are you going?' she asked, startled that he was leaving her.

'Not far. I'll be back before you're finished.'

The plunge her heart made to see him walk out of the door...

In two days that walk out of the door would be permanent, a thought that made her heart plunge even deeper.

Breathing deeply to expel the sudden distress nibbling at her and telling herself firmly not to think beyond Sunday, Kate let the manager guide her through the array of beautiful clothes and lingerie. In the end it came down to three dresses that she couldn't decide between, a handful of bras and three pairs of shoes to choose from, and the manager carried the items past an opulent waiting area and through to a dressing room that was like no dressing room she'd ever been in before. No dressing room she'd been in before was this private and plush and spacious and equipped with its own coffee machine with pods, bottles of water and a velvet sofa.

'Shall I stay and help you dress?' the manager asked.

'I'm good, thanks.' And also stark naked beneath the shirt, which wasn't a problem as it practically reached her knees but still meant there was no way she was getting undressed with a stranger in the room.

Starting with the bras, each of which she guessed must cost what she'd spent her whole lifetime on bras, Kate was dismayed to find they all fit her perfectly and all felt glorious to wear. How on earth was she supposed to decide? She'd choose one of the dresses and then make her mind up. The first dress, a silk navy number with a plunging neckline, showed way too much flesh for her liking and didn't need a bra but wanting to see it fully done up and unable to pull the zip all the way up by herself, she pressed the assistance buzzer.

In moments there was a knock on the door.

Opening it, she found Leander standing there.

His eyes locked onto hers. A sensuous smile playing on his lips, he took in the whole of her in one long sweep that sent her pulses surging. His tone one of the utmost deference and politeness, he said, 'You rang for assistance, madam?'

She had to swallow a mouth filled with moisture to say, with equal politeness, 'I need someone to do the zip up for me.'

'May I help you in this matter? Or shall I call for the manager? I'm afraid it will be a few minutes before she can attend to you.'

She cleared her throat and raised her chin. 'I'm afraid time is money and I don't have the time to wait for her.'

A knowingness gleaming in his eyes, he stepped into the dressing room and locked the door.

Giving her another long, desiring sweep, he took a step towards her and straightened. 'Turn around.'

Trembling with excitement and anticipation, Kate obeyed.

Her skin danced as his fingers plucked the zipper and slowly pulled it up.

A shiver she was helpless to do anything to stop raced up her spine. Somehow she managed to stay on her feet and turn back around to face him. 'What do you think?'

Leander didn't know what was the most beautiful aspect of the sight there before him. The melted jade of desire in Kate's eyes, the heightened colour on her cheeks, or the skimpy dress that revealed more flesh than it covered.

Lightly slipping his fingers beneath the flimsy material barely covering her breasts, he pinched the erect nipple with the exact amount of pressure guaranteed to make her moan with pleasure.

'I think,' he said huskily, kneading the whole of her breast with his palm, 'that if I take you out wearing this I'm going to be arrested for gross indecency.'

Eyes glazed, she made another mewing moan.

Placing a finger to her lips, he gently walked her backwards so her back was to the wall and rubbed his cheek against hers. 'Don't say another word,' he whispered, reaching down to her thigh and skimming his fingers under the silk and up her inner thigh to cup her naked pubis.

Theós, she was already hot and sticky for him.

Without a single word being exchanged or item of clothing removed, he used his hand and fingers to bring her to the orgasm her body was telling him she was in desperate need of. He didn't care that he would have to wait until they returned home for his own pleasure and release. Watching Kate climax was a hedonistic pleasure all in itself. Being the one to bring her to that climax...

Never had he been so fully attuned to another's needs and desires. For the first time in his life, Leander understood the pleasure that came with giving without the expectation of receiving, and as she convulsed against him, mouth pressed into his neck to stifle her moans of ecstasy, he knew he could spend the whole of his life searching and never find another Kate.

After dissolving for Leander in the dressing room, Kate had been in no fit state to try the other dresses on and so Leander had firmly insisted on taking all three of them, along with the shoes, bras and their matching knickers. After arranging for them to be delivered to the house, he then insisted on stopping for a coffee before returning home, telling her that to travel all this way without experiencing anything of life in Marina Sands was criminal.

Now, seated on the terrace of a smart little café, looking out over the ocean that was such an intrinsic part of Marina Sands, feet pressed together, they sipped coffee and spooned slices of chocolate torte.

Kate couldn't believe how happy she was. Ridiculously happy. So happy she was in danger of doing an injury to her cheek muscles.

'It's so peaceful here,' she observed.

'It is,' he agreed. 'Of all my homes, this location is one of my favourites.'

'That's a high accolade, considering the ruddy number of them.'

He grinned.

'So which one *is* your favourite?'

'Hmm… Impossible to decide. Marina Sands has the best surfing, New York has the best nightlife, Milan has the best shops. The Seychelles has the best snorkelling, Switzerland the best skiing—'

'Switzerland wasn't on my list of your properties,' she interrupted.

'I sold my original chalet last winter and only completed the purchase of the new one ten days ago.'

'Klosters?'

'Gstaad.'

'Loads of the girls at my school used to have second homes in Klosters and Gstaad.'

'Did you ever go?'

She shook her head. 'My parents hated me being at boarding school. They wanted me home every weekend and the holidays. Not that I was ever asked to go.' Only Helena had invited Kate places.

Helena's name had barely been mentioned since they'd become lovers.

'I remember you saying the school was in the next

town to your home. Why did they let you board if they hated you being away from them?'

'Because it made practical sense. The school days were long. My mum worked shifts so it would have been Dad doing all the running around.'

'She's a nurse?' Leander remembered.

'Yes.'

'And your father's an electrician?'

'Yes. By the time he'd finished work and fought through rush hour traffic, the chances of him collecting me and getting me home before seven were slim. He'd have done it gladly and we'd have made it work if I hadn't been awarded the full scholarship and had my boarding fees included. None of us expected that. The most we hoped for was to have my day fees paid for.'

'Your parents sound like amazing people.'

'They're incredible. They've supported me in everything and in so many ways. "My brothers too, even though George teased me chronically about it when we were growing up.'

'He's the brother closest to you in age?'

'An elephant would be jealous of your memory. George is three years older than me. He was always winding me up and telling me I was too thick to get the grades I needed and that I'd be lucky to get a job feeding animals. I swear, every time I opened any test or exam results, I'd imagine him laughing at me and saying *I told you so* if I'd failed.' She sniggered. 'Luckily, I was always able to wave my results in his face.'

'Luck you created with your own hard work,' he pointed out.

'But with their support, and they all made sacrifices. There is no way on this earth that I would be flying to Borneo next week if not for the sacrifices they made. I mean, I only got a full scholarship because they paid for extra tuition so I could reach the needed standard and when I was there, there were always extras that needed paying for, and then more private tuition when I was struggling with my chemistry A level. All the money to pay for that came from Mum working extra shifts and Dad taking on extra clients, and my brothers accepting without any complaints that I was being given opportunities they hadn't even dared to dream of having. They could easily have resented me but they never did. They just loved and supported me.'

'Did you become so focused on your studies because you were afraid of letting them down?' Leander asked. He just could not wrap his head around the lengths the entire Hawkins family had gone to pull together and help make the dream of a seven-year-old child come true.

She sighed and looked up at the sky. 'I think,' she said slowly, clearly thinking aloud, 'that it was fear of their sacrifices going to waste that stopped me from throwing the towel in when things got really hard. They helped keep me motivated. I suppose my dream became their dream too.'

'Do you ever think you would have chosen a different path if you weren't so scared of letting them down?'

She looked back at him with surprise at the question. 'Gosh, no. Honestly, I've never come across anything else where I've even wondered what it would be like to do. Apart from motor racing.'

He raised an eyebrow.

She grinned. My brothers are motor racing fanatics. Occasionally I'd have a wild daydream of getting behind the wheel of a Ferrari and leaving them all to dust but considering I'm a slower driver than my grandad, that's a fantasy that's never going to happen even if the opportunity arose.'

He grinned back and took her hand. 'I suppose your family is already accustomed to the day you move continents?'

'Oh, yes. They've had nearly twenty years to get used to the idea of me going. It'll still be a wrench, I know that, but we'll video call regularly and I get a return flight home for Christmas each year as part of my contract, so it's not as if I'm completely disappearing from their lives. And they can come and visit me too. We've always managed to work it out.'

'That's good.'

But it only served to remind Leander that he'd left Greece and moved continents having given his twin only a week's notice. He'd left knowing that taking his freedom would compromise their relationship but not the extent that compromise would take.

He hadn't known it would end with him losing Leo. Losing the other half of himself.

Memories suddenly flooded him from nowhere, of

all the times they'd switched identities in their child-hood, in the days before Leander had grown to resent not having an identity that was entirely his own...

Kate's toes prodded into his foot. 'Earth to Leander.'

He caught her eye and smiled ruefully. 'I was just thinking about your family having all those years to prepare for you leaving. It made me think of my parents when I took the cash and their lack of surprise. Looking back, I think they already knew what I'd do.'

'It was just Leo who hadn't known?'

Frustration had him shaking his head. 'Of course he knew. We come from the same egg. He knew me better than anyone in the world. He just refused to see or acknowledge it.'

'He might have suspected but if you didn't actually tell him...' Her words trailed off with a light but sympathetic shrug.

He drained his coffee. 'He knew but he didn't want to see.' And in truth, he *had* gone to great lengths to hide his real intentions from Leo, doing everything to delay the day when he would have to loosen the bond between them and break his brother's heart.

'And you knew but refused to say, and then when it came to the business being in trouble the roles were reversed, with Leo refusing to accept your support and you refusing to accept that he needed you to force it on him. For twins who have absolutely nothing in common, I'm getting the feeling that you both suffer from a huge dose of too much pride and stubbornness.'

For the first time since they'd become lovers Leander felt a kernel of anger unfurl at Kate. But then he saw the soft understanding in her eyes and the anger evaporated as quickly as it had formed. He'd brought the subject up, not Kate and if her observations felt a little close to the bone...

'I'm not judging you,' she said quietly, reaching over the table for his hand. 'I just think it's sad that you've lost so many years together.' Pulling his hand to her mouth, she pressed a kiss to it before a spark rang out in her stare. 'Ready to take me home, Mr Gazillionaire?'

That was better. Desire was much easier to handle than talk of ancient history, and his desire for Kate was seemingly limitless.

Kate's relief when Leander leaned over the table to kiss her and murmur, 'More than ready, my pixie princess,' was physical in its intensity. She'd seen his flare of anger at her comment over something that was, when all was said and done, none of her business.

All the same, walking back to the car, hands clasped, easy conversation flowing, she couldn't help thinking about how much courage it must have taken for Leander to pick up the phone to his brother to ask for his help last Saturday.

CHAPTER NINE

KATE WOKE TO the most delicious sensation of Leander covering her face in featherlight kisses.

'Time to wake up, sleepyhead,' he murmured, gently biting her earlobe.

Flinging her arms around him and trying to hook her legs around his waist, she was chagrined to find his arousal contained beneath a pair of shorts, and opened one eye to scowl at him.

His smile was knowing and seductive before he kissed her deeply. He tasted of toothpaste. He smelled clean.

'You had a shower without me,' she accused when he pulled his mouth from hers.

'That's because you were snoring so loudly I thought you needed the sleep,' he teased.

'Oh, no, was I doing my warthog impression?'

'You were. It was torture to my ears.' He kissed her again then shifted out of her arms and out of her reach so quickly she was forced to scowl her disappointment at him again.

Grinning, he whistled as he walked to the other end of the bedroom.

Kate lifted her head and her mood perked up to see him pick up a breakfast tray and carry it over to her. Catching the scent of bacon sent off a hunger pang and she quickly decided to wolf down the food and then get those shorts off him.

He lifted a silver lid to reveal a mound of bacon sandwiches.

She beamed her pleasure and scrambled to sit upright, holding the bedsheets under her arms so she didn't get crumbs over herself. A bacon sandwich was her all-time favourite breakfast food.

He placed the tray on her lap with a flourish and perched on the edge of the bed beside her. Along with the sandwiches were two flutes of what looked like diluted fizzy orange juice and two cups of coffee.

'Before you start...' he said, raising one of the flutes. 'To your health.'

Bemused, Kate tapped the other flute to his and, thirsty, tipped the contents down her throat. The last thing she expected was for it to contain alcohol. 'What *is* that?' she spluttered.

'Bucks Fizz,' he said smugly.

'Bucks Fizz for breakfast?'

He simply grinned, helped himself to a sandwich, and took a huge bite.

Biting into her own, Kate had another of those sensations like she'd had in the café the day before, where she'd felt she might actually burst with happiness.

Between them, they demolished the mound, and when they'd finished their drinks, Leander took the tray back to the table on the other side of the room.

Flicking the stray crumbs away, Kate threw the sheets off her and leaned back to welcome him into her arms.

That knowing, seductive gleam she so adored in his eyes, he stalked towards her but, before she could grab at him, he stopped and dug into his shorts pocket.

Her mouth fell open when he produced a square gift-wrapped box that fit perfectly in the palm of his huge hand.

Heart suddenly thrashing, she looked from the box to his gorgeous face and scrambled upright.

'Happy birthday, *agápi mou*.'

Utterly gobsmacked, she could only stare at him.

'Go on,' he chided, sitting beside her. 'Open it.'

She shook her head, not in refusal but disbelief. 'How did you know?' She'd been so caught up in the magic that was Leander that she'd barely given her birthday a thought. The times it had crossed her mind, she'd determined not to tell him, thinking it would sound needy to casually drop it into the conversation, like she was angling for a gift.

'When you mentioned being the youngest in your school year it reminded me that Helena turned down a night out with me for your birthday last year. She wouldn't let me gate-crash.' Leander had to force a smile at the memory; force it because now that he was thinking of it, it came to him all the different turns his life could have taken if he'd met Kate a year ago, before Helena had needed to get her hands on her inheritance. There would have been nothing to stop him and Kate—

Blinking the errant thought away, he added, 'I got my PA to go through my schedule for when I visited London last summer.'

She shook her head again and tucked a lock of hair behind an adorable sticky-out ear. 'Is this why you disappeared yesterday?'

'Well detected,' he said with forced lightness; this time forced because it had just dawned on him that he'd never bought a gift for a lover before. Not personally. Usually he got Sheree to do it for him.

It hadn't crossed his mind to get Sheree to organise Kate's present for him. He'd *wanted* to go into the stores and choose the perfect gift for her himself. He'd already had in mind what he would get her. It had been sheer luck that he'd found it so quickly.

'Are you going to open it or were my efforts for nothing?'

If Kate had thought she was happy before, it had nothing on the joy zipping through her veins now. Plucking the box from his hand, she tugged at the ribbon wrapped around it and carefully laid it on the bedside table. She would take it with her as another memento. Then, carefully peeling at the tiny heart-shaped sticker holding the beautiful gift-wrapping in place at its base, she flattened it out to reveal a black jewellery box.

Her heart punched into her ribs and suddenly she

found herself as terrified to look at Leander as she was to open the box.

Pulses racing madly, she pinched the tiny clasp on the box with shaking hands and had to snatch a breath before she could bring herself to open the lid.

She had no idea if it was relief or dejection that slammed into her when she caught sight of the sparkling contents.

Nestled snugly in the box was a pair of diamond stud earrings.

Leander could hardly breathe as he waited for Kate to respond. He was used to lovers being profusive in their thanks and adoration of his gifts. Too profusive. As if that was what they thought he expected. And maybe he *had* expected that kind of response. Become so used to the monetary value being praised—he was always generous with what he told Sheree to spend— that the lack of meaning behind any of the gifts hadn't mattered in the slightest.

Kate was different. This gift was different.

This gift mattered.

'I remembered you saying you didn't think it would be safe to wear anything but ear studs in your new job,' he said into the silence.

Her eyes lifted to his.

His chest tightened to see the sheen in them.

'You should be able to wear these all the time. If you want,' he added.

'Oh, I want,' she whispered. Blinking back tears, Kate gazed again at the diamonds shining so brightly under the morning light then leaned into him and palmed his stubbly cheek. 'Thank you. They're just beautiful. Perfect. I'll wear them always.'

Emotion threatening to explode out of her, she pressed her mouth to his, sliding her hand round to cup the back of his head and deepen the kiss, fighting even harder against the encroaching tears.

Kate replied to the message from the head of the plane's cabin crew and then messaged her mother.

Her heart felt so heavy she could feel its weight all the way down to her toes.

Putting her phone on the ledge, she carefully applied the mascara and lipstick she'd dug out from the bottom of her handbag and stepped back to look at herself properly.

It was for the best that they were going out, she thought morosely as she attempted a smile for the bathroom mirror. She would still be with Leander but with a new setting and probably people to help distract her from the dread that had been steadily growing in her that day. Since the messages with the flight crew started, the dread had accelerated.

Go out on a high, she told herself, giving her hair one more brush and tucking one side behind her ear. The diamond studs sparkled in her lobes. Under certain angles and lights the diamonds gave the illusion of being shaped like roses.

The earrings were simple, practical and utterly exquisite. She would cherish them for the rest of her life and try to forget that brief moment when she'd held her breath in a combination of dread and excitement that the box contained a ring.

She stepped from the bathroom to the bedroom at the same moment Leander entered the room, dressed for their night out in a tailored dark blue suit with a pale blue shirt unbuttoned at the throat.

Just the sight of him lifted her weighted heart. Kate had only seen him wear a suit once, her second night in California when she'd still believed he loathed her and had been coming to terms with her mushrooming attraction to him. She'd acknowledged to herself the suaveness of Leander in a suit but, being so intent at the time on not letting her feelings for him show, hadn't fully acknowledged the full sexiness of Leander in a suit. In truth, Leander was just sexy, whatever he wore and whatever he didn't wear. He was even sexy in his sleep.

She was going to miss him desperately.

His gleaming dark eyes slowly looked her up and down. He gave a low whistle. '*Theós*, Kate. You look wonderful.'

All she needed was a crown to sit on her blonde hair and she'd be his pixie princess come to life, Leander thought, although he was quite sure pixies weren't famed for being irresistibly sexy. He could laugh. Of the three dresses from the boutique, she'd chosen to wear the least revealing of them. Created with large black and red embroidered roses interlinked with red lace, the long-sleeved dress scooped across her collarbone and fell to just above her knees. On her feet were sandals held together with a thin black strap across the toes and another around her ankles. The heels were high enough to elevate her so the top of her head almost reached his chin. Without them, she barely reached his shoulders.

The least revealing dress and already his loins were tightening with anticipation of stripping it off her.

Kate could wear sackcloth and she'd still be irresistible to him.

About to haul her into his arms and show her just how irresistible she was, he caught a bleakness in her stare. 'What's wrong?'

She gave a tight-lipped smile and a small shrug. 'I need to leave earlier than I thought tomorrow.'

'When?'

'I need to be in the air by eleven.'

There was a sinking sensation in the pit of his stomach. 'In the morning?' They'd made loose plans to leave for Europe simultaneously late afternoon.

She nodded forlornly. 'I'd forgotten to factor in the time difference between California and England. I'm being collected at ten. If my flight leaves here by eleven, I'll land around five Monday morning British time. I'll be lucky to make it home before six. I'll only have a few hours left to sort myself out before I head back to the airport and I've got so much I need to do and people to say goodbye to.' Another forlorn smile. 'I knew all the travelling I did coming to find you had screwed my sense of time but hadn't realised how badly.'

Finding his lungs had tightened, Leander stroked her soft cheek and grazed a kiss to her sweet mouth, inhaling the scent of her skin to loosen his airways. They'd known from the outset that their time together was limited so it was futile to waste the hours they had left envisaging the moment they had to say goodbye. 'It is only a few hours earlier. If we forget about sleeping tonight we won't lose any time.'

Her lips relaxed into a smile against his. 'I like your way of thinking.'

He slid a hand around her slender back to clasp a peachy buttock. 'And I like that you like it.' Not wanting to ruin her lipstick, he restrained himself to another light kiss before taking her hand and stepping back. 'Come on, birthday girl. Let's go and celebrate while the night is still young.'

Leander sat in the back of the car with Kate's hand clasped in his, her head resting against his shoulder and her sweet scent filling his senses, trying to tune out that this was their last night together. Trying but not succeeding.

The healing wound on her knee was a reminder of how close he'd come to escaping her. If she hadn't tripped, he would have got in his car. He would never have experienced the hedonistic joy of making love to her.

Someone else would have shared her first time with her.

As some point in her future, someone else would take his place.

He wanted that for her, he told himself firmly. Kate had an earthy, sexual side to her nature and now that it had been unleashed, it was unreasonable to imagine she would leave California and be satisfied with a life of celibacy.

For all that he tried to make himself sound reasonable in his own thoughts, Leander didn't deny that knowing she'd be living and working in such a remote location and so would have limited opportunities to meet potential lovers made it easier to have his reasonable thoughts, but that only set his mind racing to her colleagues, the people she would live and work with. What if one of them swept Kate off her feet? A likeminded colleague she could have not only as a lover but build a life with. Maybe marry. Have children...

'You're hurting my hand.' Kate's murmured voice cut through his thoughts.

Realising he'd been squeezing too tightly, he immediately loosened his hold and kissed her delicate fingers in apology. 'Sorry.'

Concern shone in her eyes. 'Are you okay? You've been very quiet.'

He forced a smile. 'Just exercising my brain cells... and we're almost there. Look.'

Figuring that he'd share what was on his mind in his own time, not daring to think that time might have run out for them before that happened, Kate followed his stare. Excitement pushed much of the melancholy out of her and she opened her window to see more clearly, taking in the enormous fairground on the pier they were passing far to her left, the high rides aglow in neon colours illuminating the dark. She could almost hear the screams of the thrill-seekers, practically taste the scent of doughnuts and candyfloss.

Exactly twenty minutes after they'd set out from Leander's home, the driver took a right turn onto a wide street lined by high buildings with architecture that made her think of Spanish cities and soon they were crawling down what was obviously a theatre district, the pavements packed with people in various guises of dress, from haute couture to wacky, a smorgasbord of visual delight.

The car stopped.

'We're going to watch a show?' Kate asked.

He tapped her nose lightly. 'In a way. You'll see.'

Stepping out of the car and breathing in the energy of the place was enough to zap the last of the melancholy out of her.

This was her last night with Leander. It was her birthday. What kind of masochist would she be if she didn't make the most of every last minute with him?

Grinning, she raised herself onto her toes and planted a kiss to his mouth. 'Thank you.'

'Don't thank me yet—you don't know where we're going.'

'I don't have to know that to know I'll enjoy it.' Leander had taken her to a variety of places during her time on his family's Greek island and she'd loved all of them. Loved them because he'd been with her with his infectious good humour. Leander could take her on a date to an academic library and she'd still adore every moment.

'No pressure for me then,' he observed with a flash of his teeth, taking hold of her hand.

With a giggle, she happily let him lead her to a narrow arched door that, in comparison to the other doors along this street, was nondescript, a simple non-neon flashing sign above it in italics: *Trevis*. Leander had his phone ready and showed whatever was expected to a burly bouncer who nodded them through with wishes for them to have a good evening.

There was nothing nondescript about the interior.

There was a fleeting moment when Kate thought she'd travelled back in time and that Marilyn Monroe or Audrey Hepburn or Bette Davis would sashay down the golden cantilevered stairs, a sense that if she breathed in hard enough she'd be able to smell decades-old cigars and Scotch.

Around them, treading on the thick maroon carpet, were dozens of people dressed so glamorously she could believe they were at a movie awards ceremony. Everything in this reception room screamed glamour, from the golden chandeliers to the art deco artwork to the waiting staff hovering semi discreetly with trays of canapés and champagne.

Catching Leander's stare, she laughed. 'What *is* this place?'

'A private theatre.'

'So we *are* watching a show?'

He grinned, caught the eye of a waitress and plucked two flutes of champagne from her tray. After tapping their glasses together, he led Kate through the milling crowd and down wide marble steps into a vast auditorium. Where rows of seats would normally be at the front of the stage were dozens and dozens of tables already filled with yet more glamorous people.

An official greeted them. After Leander again showed his phone, they were taken to a table for two only feet away from the stage.

What followed was the most surreal yet entertaining show Kate had ever been to, an immersive mystical acrobatic cabaret like nothing she'd ever seen, with black magic and comedy that made her gasp and laugh and hide behind her hands, often all at the same time. Throughout it, course after course of beautifully presented and delicious-tasting food, champagne and cocktails were served to them. Kate was so enthralled with what was happening both on the stage and above them that she could have been eating cardboard for all the attention she paid to it.

By the time the finale came, she was giddy with the joy of it all and so at first didn't realise that the acrobat dressed as a water nymph swinging on a giant gold hoop suspended from the ceiling held a cake in her nimble hands, not until the hoop was lowered and the nymph, to loud screams of delight from the audience, swung upside down and expertly dropped the cake on their table. She had barely clocked the iced *Happy Birthday Kate* inscription and array of candles before the *pièce de résistance* came. For as long as Kate lived, she would never work out how she did it but the nymph exhaled and lit the candles with her breath of fire.

To see the awed wonder on Kate's face made the hours Leander was forgoing that could have been spent in bed with her worth it. To have those jade eyes lock with his and feel the emotion shining from them...

She kissed him on the mouth. 'Thank you,' she said reverently, squeezing his fingers threaded through hers.

He kissed her back. 'My pleasure. Blow your candles out.'

Smoothing her hair away from her face, she extinguished the candles with one long breath then beamed at him and shook her head. 'How did you do all this?'

He gave a modest shrug that made her laugh. 'However you pulled it off, thank you.'

'I don't sleep as much as you,' he teased by way of explanation.

Her eyes gleamed. 'Then you must be running on no sleep at all.'

'The time we've had together has been worth any lost sleep.'

'I'll drink to that.' She lifted her cocktail to him.

Clinking his champagne to it, they finished their drinks in unison.

Glasses placed back on the table, Leander covered

her hand and leaned his face close to hers. 'I wanted to give you a night to remember me by.' As he spoke, the sinking sensation in his stomach of earlier returned and it took all his control not to let his fingers tighten their grip on her delicate hand the way they reflexively wanted to.

Soon, this delicate hand would be working on giant apes and the hardworking, learned brain in Kate's beautiful head fully focused on her orphaned orange patients, and he, Leander, would be nothing but a distant memory to her.

He'd never felt the need to create memories with anyone before.

The lightness of her features dimmed a touch before she laughed. 'Then consider your plan a success because this is easily the best night out I've ever had and hands down the best birthday.'

All around them, the crowd rose, clapping and whistling enthusiastically as the performers took to the stage for the adulation and applause they'd worked so hard for, and Kate rose with them. Putting her fingers in her mouth, she wolf-whistled loudly and grinned widely at Leander's admiration, her grin almost splitting her face when he put his own fingers in his mouth and followed suit.

The giddy joy of the evening had turned into a fizzing sensation in her veins, and when Leander asked if she wanted to check out the private nightclub on the top floor and she glanced at the time and saw they still had a maximum twelve hours left together, she happily clutched his hand and walked with him back into the reception and up the cantilevered stairs.

The top floor was a warren of corridors and doors but the nightclub was easy to find by following the throbbing music.

Kate could feel the throbs deep in her fizzing veins and when they entered the darkened room with its glamorous maroon and gold sensual vibe, and they both drank a glass of champagne before heading onto the hardwood floor, she wound her arms around Leander's neck and thought that if she hadn't had that minor panic attack before her final exams and begged off that night out with Helena and so met Leander back then, her life might have taken a very different direction.

He wouldn't have been promised to Helena then. Kate would have met him safe in the knowledge that Helena was playing cupid. Her time at university almost over, she would have looked at him with her mind already open to possibilities, and she'd have been sunk. She saw that clearly. If she'd met Leander back when Helena had tried to fix them up, she would have found him irresistible from the off. She saw clearly, too, that if he'd fixed those dark brown eyes on her the way they were fixed on her now, she would have fallen for him. He would have filled her opened mind to the point where he was all she could think about and she would have failed her finals.

And if he'd taken her dancing and held her the way he was holding her now, with the scent of his warm skin and cologne darting through her senses, she would have fallen in love with him and given up her dreams of Borneo to be his for ever.

CHAPTER TEN

THE DANCE FLOOR of the private nightclub was packed. Leander wasn't complaining. It meant he was forced to keep Kate and her hot little body close.

With their bodies grinding together to the deep R&B beats pulsing through the floor and Kate's arms hooked around his neck, arousal thrummed strongly in him.

Arousal always thrummed with Kate.

He could do nothing to stop it firing into his loins.

Tightening the clasp on her bottom, he ground her against him, letting her feel his hardness.

Her lips parted in a throaty exhale, the jade of her eyes melting with the same heat that heightened the colour on her cheeks. Fingers of one hand slipped under the collar of his shirt, the other skipping down his arm and tightening around his back.

Eyes and pelvises locked, their bodies continued the sensual grind to the music, desire flowing in a current that grew stronger with every passing beat.

Theós, he'd never known it was possible to want someone so much, for arousal to infect every atom of your body, for the want to multiply with every coupling. Never known he was susceptible to addiction.

Two weeks ago he'd collected Kate from his family's airfield. The roof of his car had been down. Helena had sat in the front, Kate in the back. Kate had poked her head between them and asked him to turn the music up because a song was playing that she liked. Before they'd had a proper conversation they'd sung along, badly, to a tune he knew he would spend the rest of his life thinking of Kate whenever he heard it. By the time they'd arrived at his family's home, a strong friendship had established itself.

He'd never had that with a woman before. Helena didn't count because Helena was like family to him.

He'd been addicted to Kate's company before he was even aware of wanting her. He'd not allowed himself to see her as a woman because she was only there to act the role of maid of honour for his fake marriage and then when the blinkers had come off his eyes as Dimitri had leered all over her, the depth of his want had scared the hell out of him.

He could never have imagined those two short and yet so long weeks ago that he would find himself addicted to making love to her. Addicted to the sound of her voice, her laugh, her smile. Kate Hawkins touched something in him that no one had touched before and when her nails dug into his neck and she rose onto her toes to breathily whisper in his ear, 'Is there somewhere private we can go?' the pulse that shot through him almost brought him to his knees.

Spearing her hair, he gazed deep into her eyes. The meaning of her words reflected in their liquid depths.

Hands clasped tightly, desire thrumming like an infection in his blood, he led her through the heaving bodies on the dance floor and out of the nightclub room. The first two doors in the corridor were locked. The third opened into an empty, perfumed, sensuous cloakroom with a maroon leather sofa and mirrored walls.

The burning ache inside Kate meant she didn't hesitate. Locking the door, she pushed Leander against the wall and pulled his head down to her. Devouring his mouth with all the passion she possessed…she felt like *she* was possessed…she yanked his shirt free and set to work on freeing him. The moment his erection was released she dropped to her knees, gripped the base and closed her lips around him.

His groan of pleasure fed the ache in her.

Too big to fit whole in her mouth, she used her hand along with her tongue and lips to pleasure him, thrilling at his moans and the way his big hands held her head, the pads of his fingers clasping her skull without restricting her. His groan when she cupped his balls was guttural. Lifting her stare, she found his hooded eyes on her, his features ablaze.

'*Theós*, Kate, what are you doing to me?' he muttered hoarsely before closing his eyes and throwing his head back.

Loving you, she would have replied if her mouth hadn't been full.

Loving Leander. The most natural, beautiful, intoxicating feeling in the world. What he'd done for her that night, the effort he'd gone to…

This might be the last chance she'd have to show what it all meant to her. What *he* meant to her.

He meant everything. For Kate, Leander had become everything.

How was she supposed to say goodbye to him? She couldn't. It couldn't end like this. There had to be a way…

Although Kate had pleasured Leander with her mouth before, it had never felt like this, like the pleasure could split him into atoms. Release had never felt so necessary but as heady as it felt to reach climax this way, there was no single pleasure greater than finding release buried inside her.

Sensing the point of no return speeding towards him, he tightened his grip on her head and tilted her face. 'Come here,' he said thickly.

Her arms were wound back around his neck and her hot mouth on his in moments.

Twisting her around so it was Kate's back to the wall, he slid a hand up her thigh and clasped her bare bottom.

Theós, and he'd thought he'd been close to coming before?

'No underwear?'

She grinned into his mouth before her tongue continued its dance with his.

He didn't hesitate. Lifting her up, he thrust straight into the tight confines of her sticky heat.

Her legs wrapped around his waist, Kate closed her eyes and clung tightly to him as he pounded into her, softly moaning as she extracted every ounce of the pleasure Leander was giving them both.

So hot and ready was she for him that her climax came quickly and she clung even tighter, closing her eyes as the waves of ecstasy shot through her, trying to drown out the thought that it was now Sunday and that very soon she would have to say goodbye to all of this.

She would have to say goodbye to the love of her life.

Kate flopped into Leander's arms in the back of the car and blew a lock of hair off her face.

What a night. The most fun, magical night of her life. The best birthday of her life.

Shifting to make herself comfortable, she nestled her head under his chin and stroked the hand resting under her breasts. She closed her eyes and expelled a contented sigh. His breath was warm in her hair. She could feel the rhythmic thumps of his heart through her back...

'Wake up, sleepyhead, we're home.'

Blinking herself back to life, she jerked upright and was astounded to find they'd reached the top of Leander's private drive.

In another blink, all the joy and contentment drained from her.

She'd just wasted twenty minutes with Leander

sleeping. A quick look at her watch showed there were only eight hundred minutes left. Her car was collecting her at ten a.m. It had just turned two.

'Take a shower with me?' he asked knowingly after they'd stepped inside and he'd thrown his phone into his study.

She tried to coax her lips into the beaming smile that had been ever present since she'd made the decision to stay, but this time it was an effort. Making her legs bounce up the stairs to his bedroom was an effort. The only thing that was no effort at all was stripping herself naked, stepping into Leander's walk-in shower and making love to him. This time she tried to draw the pleasure out for as long as she could but her body was so responsive to his touch that her climax came as quickly as it had in the nightclub...and when it did come, the usual separation from her body failed to happen and instead of crying out her bliss she found herself pressing her mouth tightly against his neck to stop herself from crying tears.

After he'd wrapped her in a big fluffy towel and carried her to his bed, they made love again, and even though the pleasure was drawn out this time and her climax as powerful as she'd ever experienced, still she couldn't find the separation she so desperately sought, still she fought back tears.

The worst bit was afterwards, lying in Leander's arms, exhaustion trying to lull her into wasting more of her precious time with him in sleep.

Rubbing at her tired eyes, she sat up. 'Can I have a coffee?'

His smile was half sad, half knowing. 'Extra strong and extra sweet?'

Her heart filling that he knew she needed the caffeine and sugar dose to stave off the sleepiness, she nodded.

The coffee was delivered to Leander's room soon after. The night's weather was for once relatively balmy so they took it out onto his balcony, Leander in a pair of shorts he hadn't bothered doing the button up on and Kate in one of his sweaters that, like all the other items of his clothing she'd borrowed, she had no intention of giving back to him.

She would take every memento she could. She might make a shrine to him with it all, she thought, trying to jolly herself along with absurd thoughts.

The balcony had a small round iron table and two chairs on it. Sitting beside him, she slung her legs over his lap and fingered her earrings. At least she would always have something of Leander as a part of her, she told herself valiantly, then looked out over the black sky and the dotted white crests of the ocean reflecting off the stars, and breathed in the salty but sweet night air. The ocean was calm that night, the usually loud crash of waves hitting the beach muted.

Not even Leander's hand stroking her thigh could soothe the crash of Kate's heart hitting her ribs or stop the hand holding her coffee cup from shaking.

This would be the last time she'd share the same

night sky as him. When the sun rose it would be the last daybreak she'd share with him.

How could she bear it?

She'd thought she was prepared but now, with time picking up speed and the moment of her departure less than six hours away…

Time was slipping away from her and with every second that passed, the ache in her heart spread.

'You're very quiet,' Leander observed. Kate hadn't spoken a word since they'd sat down and was now on her second cup of coffee. There was a tension in her body that had never been there before.

She finished her drink and leaned over to put the cup on the table. 'Just exercising my brain cells,' she said, mimicking his earlier comment. If the night wasn't so still and Leander so attuned to her, he wouldn't have noticed the tiny choke in her voice.

Gently lifting her chin with his finger, he gazed down into eyes that shone with misery.

For a long moment they just stared at each other and then her pretty heart-shaped chin wobbled and a tear rolled down her cheek. 'I can't do this,' she whispered with a quiet sob.

Leander closed his eyes and pulled in a breath as he wrapped his arms around her. Kissing the top of her silky hair, he kept his mouth there and fought the swell of emotions her tear had let loose in him.

For another long moment they stayed locked as they were, with Kate's wet cheek against his chest and her small hand gripping his bicep, Leander's mouth on her head and his hands stroking her back. Her slender body was trembling.

A long time passed before she disentangled herself to look back at him. It was as if her whole face had crumpled. 'How am I supposed to say goodbye to you? I *can't.*'

The pain in his chest was like nothing he'd felt before. 'You can and you will. It has to be this way.'

More tears filled her eyes and she shook her head. 'It *doesn't.*'

'It does. We always knew it would have to end.' They'd been over before they'd even started.

Her voice was barely audible. 'I didn't know it would hurt so much.'

He hadn't known either.

Lightly, tenderly, he stroked her cheek. 'It hurts now but in a few days you'll be in Borneo. This is it, Kate. Your dream is coming to life, and when you're there you'll be so busy that the pain will fade to nothing.'

'Is that how it was for you when you left your brother?' she whispered.

The pain in his chest sharpened. 'That was different, and I didn't leave Leo.' Ultimately, Leo had left *him*.

Her swimming eyes held his before she blinked sharply and her back straightened. 'I can wait for you.'

Unsure what she was suggesting, he stared into her eyes.

Fevered animation suddenly lit her face. 'The two things stopping us being together are your promise to Helena and me moving to Borneo. I don't have to go to

Borneo. Well, I do, but I don't have to stay. You need to go back to Greece and play the role of Helena's husband and help her get her inheritance but that'll take a few months to sort out, which is enough time for the charity to find a replacement for me, and then we can—'

Hardly able to believe what she was saying, he cut her off. 'Kate, stop.'

'But this is the perfect solution, don't you see? Helena will be happy for us, we both know that, and I'll still get a few months in Borneo and then—'

'Are you seriously suggesting that you would give up the job you've spent your whole life working for, for *me*?'

Jade eyes bright, she nodded.

Nausea rolled violently in his guts. God help him, she *was* serious.

Thinking hard and quickly through the nausea and the roar of blood in his head, Leander tried to find the angle needed to make Kate see that what she was suggesting was impossible.

She was prepared to give up everything for him. Give up everything for the man who'd destroyed his own brother in pursuit of his own selfish needs.

He could not let her do that.

'And your family?' he asked, stalling.

'They will understand.'

'Kate…' He filled his lungs with air and hardened himself to speak the words that would set the ball rolling for the first unselfish act he would make in his life. 'You can't do that.'

'I promise you, if I'm happy then they're happy.' That was one thing Kate was quite sure of. 'They made all those sacrifices for me because they love me and want me to be happy.' It had been her own fears of wasting their sacrifices that had driven her forwards when she would otherwise have given up. Thanks to them, she'd reached the finish line of her marathon. The destination she took now didn't have to be fixed in stone. 'And I'm sure they'd secretly be happier if I got a job somewhere a little less remote. I can start my own small practice or work for another zoo or—'

'Have you forgotten my aversion to long-term relationships?' Leander cut in. 'You would be throwing away your dreams for a man who doesn't want to make a commitment to anything permanent.'

Confusion clouded her beautiful features. 'But...' Her voice trailed away for a moment. 'Don't you want to try? There's lots of ways we can make it work. I'd give up Borneo for you but there could be a way for us to be together without me having to do that, and—'

Loathing himself for the hurt he was inflicting on her, a hurt that lanced his own heart, Leander had no choice but to inflict more of it. 'What we have shared these last few days has been great, but I haven't said anything that would make you think I want more than this.'

The last of the brightness and animation vanished. Her voice was stark. Bewildered. 'You're happy to never see me again?'

He couldn't tell her a bare-faced lie of that magnitude. 'I wouldn't say I was *happy* about it.'

The bewilderment of her voice was mirrored in her eyes. 'Then what? Why are you being like this?'

'We became lovers knowing—both of us—that our time here was all we could have.'

'That was then, and you can't expect me to believe after everything we've shared that you're happy for us to be over.'

'I just said I wasn't happy about it, but lust is a powerful emotion.'

She flinched as if he'd physically wounded her. 'Lust?'

'Lust,' he confirmed firmly, confirming it to them both. Leander's feelings for Kate were stronger than anything he'd believed it was possible to feel and he'd known from the moment they became lovers that saying goodbye to her would be a wrench, but that wasn't reason enough to let her throw away her life's work on something that would never last and for a man like him, someone selfish, who put his own needs and wants above those he loved. 'And the lust between us is strong. You're only feeling like this because our time together has been short and we haven't had the chance to work it out of our systems. There is no way to make it work between us that doesn't involve one of us giving up the things most precious to us and the end result would still be the same, whichever one of us made the sacrifices necessary—our desire for each other coming to a natural end. I'm not built for sustaining a relationship.'

He watched the colour drain from her face and thought he had never hated himself so much.

There was truth in being cruel to be kind, he thought grimly. And truth in the truth hurting.

'You don't mean that,' she whispered.

'I do mean it. You know me, Kate. You know the kind of man I am. I am sorry if your feelings have changed, but mine haven't. I think the world of you but we wouldn't have a future together even if Borneo wasn't a factor.'

CHAPTER ELEVEN

KATE HAD TO fight the painful ripples of her thundering heart to focus on what was radiating from Leander's eyes. There was a hardness in them she hadn't seen since the days before they'd become lovers. It was a hardness he'd deliberately adopted to drive her away. If not for her tripping over, he would have succeeded. She would not let him succeed now.

She couldn't. Just to imagine it…

'I do know the kind of man you are,' she said slowly, not dropping her stare, knowing the second she lost her focus then the panic that had been building inside her since they'd arrived back at his home would take control of her. It had already come close to doing just that and with time accelerating at the same rate as the panic, she knew she had to keep her head together and fight, however hard, for both their sakes. 'And that's why I don't believe you.'

His jaw tightened, an edge coming into his voice. 'As you pointed out less than a week ago, I'm known as Leander the Lothario for a reason.'

She covered his hand and meditatively said, 'You

ran away from Greece and your wedding to Helena because of your feelings for me.'

His hand tensed beneath her touch. The edge deepened. 'I didn't run away. I needed time and space to get my head together.'

'Because of your feelings for me.'

The bones of his jaw were straining against his stubbly skin. 'No, for my conscience. How could I make vows to someone if it was the maid of honour I wanted to bed?'

If she wasn't feeling so wretchedly sick, she would laugh. 'Your conscience didn't stop you agreeing to marry Helena to begin with though, did it? It didn't bother you that you would be making vows that were lies. You thought it would be *fun* to marry her, and let's be brutally honest here, you've bedded so many women that I'd be a fool if I thought I was the only woman attending the wedding you would have taken up with given the chance.'

Yanking his hand away, he pushed her legs off him and got abruptly to his feet. 'I'm trying to do the right thing here, Kate,' he said, pacing away from her. 'I would give anything to have more time with you, but our time has run out and now we must go our separate ways. You need to accept that.'

'How can I?' she asked starkly. Rising unsteadily to her own feet, she fought with everything she had to keep the panic controlled and her voice calm. 'The thought of leaving you behind and never seeing you again is *killing* me and I know it's hurting you too.'

He lifted his head and breathed in deeply through his nose. 'Nothing lasts for ever, not hurt and not lust. Lust always burns itself out.'

'We feel more for each other than lust and you know it.'

Features unreadable, he opened the patio door. 'I think it's time to end this conversation before words are said that cannot be taken back.'

'We are way past that point, Leander. The toothpaste has already been squeezed out.'

He moved so swiftly that he caught her off-guard, one moment standing at the threshold of his bedroom, the next his hands on her shoulders, leaning down so his taut face was right against hers. 'I don't want to hurt you, Kate,' he said roughly, nostrils flaring, 'but when you leave here, that is it for us. You have to accept it. Move on and embrace your new life—God knows you deserve it after all those years of hard work.'

Seeing the implacability in his eyes shifted something in Kate. All these hours, time had been slipping away from her and now it was Leander himself. For the first time she understood on a cellular level that she was losing him and when he let go of her shoulders and made to step away, desperation had her snatching hold of his wrist. 'Stop making it sound as if you're doing me a favour and that I'm the one who needs to be all reasonable and accepting when you're the one who won't accept the truth. You *know* we've found something special—'

'Oh, I know it, do I?' Leander interrupted as blood that had been slowly filling with something that felt very much like fury at Kate's refusal to accept things the way they were meant to be suddenly surged to his head. He had done nothing wrong except fail to follow some sad script Kate had written in her head where she expected him to declare his undying love and embrace a future he had never wanted and had never lied about not wanting. 'Did sharing my bed give you magical mind-reading abilities?'

Her hold on his wrist tightened and her despairing face drew even closer. 'I don't need magical powers to know you've spent so many years hiding from human relationships that you'd rather throw away what we have than deal with your feelings for me.'

He only realised his hands were still clasping her shoulders when he had to fight to stop himself from shaking them. 'You don't know what you're talking about. I've never hidden from anything in my life.'

A visible shot of anger merged with the despair. 'You've been hiding from emotions since you were eighteen and told Leo you weren't going to join the business with him,' she said, disbelief in her voice. 'You waited until the last minute to throw that bombshell at him and because you knew how much it would devastate him, you ran away rather than deal with the wreckage that *you* created, and you've been running ever since. You wouldn't even go home when the business was in trouble and he needed you most...'

'He didn't *want* me to go home,' he reminded her angrily.

'Stop lying to yourself,' she cried. 'He didn't need

your help but he needed *you*—just you, and if you would just take your blinkers off for two minutes you'd see that you need him too. But you've been so intent on proving to yourself that you don't need anyone and that you're more than just one of the Liassidis twins and that breaking your own twin's heart was worth it, that you won't admit how much you miss him or admit that you've effectively shut out anyone from getting close to you again. Properly close, I mean. Only people like Helena are safe for you to love because they don't expect more than you're prepared to give.'

The dark, dangerous fury on Leander's face, an expression far beyond anything she'd seen before, was enough to make a sane person quail but in that moment, Kate was far from sane. It felt like only minutes ago that he'd been making love to her in the shower, only seconds since he'd tenderly wrapped a big fluffy towel around her, a mere beat since he'd touched the diamond studs in her ears and then kissed her as if she were the most precious thing in his world.

'If I hadn't come with an end date attached, you would never have made love to me,' she continued, uncaring that she was close to shouting now. 'You'd have carried on running because that's what you were doing when you escaped from Greece and broke your promise to Helena and then treated me so cruelly—running from your feelings for me. Well, I've spent my whole life running too, so damn determined to be a vet and fulfil a dream that came to me when I was a *child* and so frightened of letting my family down after everything they'd done for me that the only friendship I ever properly embraced until you came along was with Helena. Learning was so hard for me and I was so frightened of anything distracting me like it did with Euan that I developed a tunnel vision I didn't even realise I'd become trapped in. *You* smashed that tunnel down, Leander, and for the first time I can see how dreams can voluntarily be broken and discarded because being loved by you is the best feeling in the whole world. But now I ruddy well wish I hadn't tripped on that stupid step because tripping pushed me into falling in love with you and now I've got to face the rest of my life knowing the love of my life is at heart a selfish bastard who—'

Kate's unplanned diatribe came to a sudden halt when Leander clasped the hand gripping his wrist and brought his face so close to hers that the tips of their noses touched. 'If you'd been paying the slightest bit of attention you would know I'm not a man to break dreams over,' he said quietly but harshly. 'I didn't ask for your love. I didn't ask for any of this. I came here to get my head together without any distractions so I could fulfil my promise to Helena. You forced your way in and refused to leave. If you hadn't lived your life shunning relationships you would know that sharing a man's bed doesn't make him magically fall in love with you, and now I think it's best that you leave.'

Prising her fingers off his wrist, he dropped her hand and stepped into his room.

Moments later she heard him speaking on the intercom. 'Please bring a car to the front. Miss Hawkins is leaving.'

The white noise in her head was so dizzyingly powerful that she had to grab the side of a chair to stop herself from falling.

Somehow, she managed to stagger inside.

Seeing Leander shrugging a shirt on through the open door of his dressing room made her rapidly bruising heart thump painfully. He'd already replaced his shorts with a pair of black jeans.

'Don't do this,' she whispered, clutching the door frame.

Fingers working deftly on the shirt buttons, he fixed his implacable stare on her. 'Get your stuff together. Mason is going to drive you to the airfield. I suggest you call the flight crew so they can prepare.'

'Please, Leander.'

Leander blurred Kate's tear-stained face from his vision. He'd always known their parting would be painful and had prepared himself mentally for it. The only aspect he hadn't foreseen and prepared for was Kate's devastation. *Theós*, it hurt to witness it, hurt enough that he already forgave her ridiculous amateur psychoanalysis of him.

One day she would understand that he'd acted for the best, that he'd been thinking about her best interests as much as his own.

'Assure Helena that I will be back in Greece at some point tonight,' he said stiffly as he tucked the shirt into his jeans.

'Leander, *please*.'

Clenching his jaw at her audible pain, he strode past her, making sure not a cell of his body brushed against her. From his bedside table he picked up his thick Omega watch and secured it to his wrist. 'I have work I need to catch up on before I leave.'

'*Leander*.'

Leander caught Kate's stare one last time. 'I wish you well with your new life. Embrace it, Kate, and forget about me.'

And then he left his room and strode the mezzanine to the stairs. On the ground floor he entered his study for the first time since he'd arrived in Marina Sands and locked the door behind him.

Only when he'd sunk into his office chair did he expel the breath he hadn't even been aware of holding and cradle his head in his hands.

Cheek pressed against the car window, Kate cuddled her handbag tightly to her heaving chest. Tears she had no control over blinded her so greatly she didn't notice they'd left Leander's land until they'd made the turn onto the main road and flashing lights broke the darkness. The driver beeped his horn at a driver trying to squeeze into a gap between vehicles lined on the verge and making a right mess of it, but she didn't have the energy to care about what they were there for or care why some of their owners had flashed their cameras at her car.

She'd never imagined pain like this existed.

Had she really got it all wrong? Had she only imagined that Leander's feelings for her ran as deeply as hers did for him? Had it really been nothing but naive wishful thinking on her part?

The road her driver was taking her on that early morning was the coastal route. On the horizon, the first glimmer of light.

Closing her eyes, she breathed deeply in a vain effort to stifle the agony ripping through her that Leander had snatched their last sunrise together away from her.

He hadn't even left his study to say goodbye. The last words he'd said to her were *'forget about me'*.

How could she do that when he'd brought her more joy than she'd experienced during the rest of her life combined?

She couldn't.

Spotting a sign for Marina Sands Boulevard through the car's headlights only hit her with memories of their one shopping trip. He'd sneaked away to buy her the earrings…

The earrings were still in her ears. She was still wearing his sweater. She'd failed to take any of her other mementoes. Had forgotten all about them. The agony of knowing she would never see him again had taken her over. She'd barely made it through the conversation with the flight crew, and thinking of this came with a vague recollection of seeing a missed call and voicemail notification on her phone.

Snatching at the needed distraction, Kate rubbed furiously at her eyes and pulled her phone out of her bag.

The nausea that had been simmering in her belly bubbled higher when she realised the missed call was from Helena and that it had been left six hours ago at midnight.

She put the phone to her ear.

From the first spoken syllable, she knew something terrible had happened.

'Kate, the press know.' Helena's panicked voice rang out. 'Please, *please* be careful. They're everywhere and they'll be looking for you and Leander too…' A sound like a sob being stifled. 'I'm so sorry for dragging you into this. I'm sorry for everything. I should have known…' Another stifled sob. 'Please forgive me.'

The voicemail ended.

Leander knew he shouldn't watch Kate being driven away from him. He knew it and still he did it, standing at the window long after the car's lights had disappeared, still standing there as the first rays of the dawn's light penetrated the darkness. For all he knew, he could have stood there for ever, haunted by Kate's complete desolation, if his phone hadn't rung loudly.

It was the ringtone he used for his PA.

No point in ignoring it. Today he must return to his real life and fulfil the promise he'd made.

There was a lethargy in his limbs that made him fumble to answer it and which carried through to his tired voice. 'Yes, Sheree?'

'Oh, thank God. I've been trying to reach you for hours.'

'Have you?' he asked dully. How many hours had

passed since he'd put his phone in the study when he'd returned to the house so there was no chance of his last night with Kate being interrupted? It felt like a lifetime. It felt like no time at all.

Sheree cut straight to the chase. 'There are date and time-stamped pictures of you and a woman who isn't Helena kissing in a theatre. They were taken last night.'

He pinched the bridge of his nose. 'Tell the press it's Leo.'

'They know it's you. A Greek blogger has been touring the Californian homes of famous Greeks for a series he's doing.'

'What?'

'You know the kind of blog I mean.' He dimly imagined the eyeroll she made at this. 'He located your home and it's your bad luck that he found it and was about to try his luck and explore the grounds when you drove past him with a blonde lady. He thought the place would be empty, seeing as you're supposed to be in Greece on your honeymoon.'

Leander swore under his breath.

'He followed you into the city last night and when he saw where you'd gone, found the staff entrance and bribed an usher on a break to get pictures of the two of you. The pictures were enough for the press to run with it. They've been looking at flight manifests and know that you're the Liassidis twin in California and that Leo is still in Greece. They know Leo is masquerading as you. The only way to deny this is to play it that Leo used your passport to enter the US, which is highly likely to be a federal offence.'

'We can't do that,' he said automatically. The weight that had been in his heart since he'd watched Kate drive away had sunk to his toes and filled his every crevice.

In one night he'd destroyed the three people who meant the most to him. If he'd ever held an iota of hope that he and Leo could one day rebuild their relationship then this would be its death knell. He doubted Helena would forgive him either. He wouldn't forgive himself if he was in their shoes.

This was everything Kate had warned him about.

It was almost ironic that he hadn't been recognised as himself but through his home.

'I've got extra security coming to you. They should be with you any minute.'

'Thank you. See that Kate has security when she arrives back in England.'

'That's the blonde?'

His hackles rose at this casual, dismissive observation. 'Yes,' he answered shortly, well aware the dismissive observation came from Sheree having spent a decade dealing with a myriad of Leander's lovers who never stuck around long enough for her to get on first name terms with. 'I'll send you her details. Tell them it might be necessary to travel to Borneo with her.'

He couldn't be with her but he could keep her safe until she reached the safety of the Borneo rainforest.

No sooner had he put the phone down than it rang

again. A different ringtone. One he'd programmed when he'd bought the phone new but had never rung.

It was the ringtone for his brother.

For the first time in five years, Leo was calling him.

Kate couldn't bring herself to leave the car. The jet's steps had been lowered, two members of the cabin crew at the opened door ready to welcome her in, and all she could do was stare at the photos of herself and Leander sharing a kiss and the headlines screaming about the Liassidis twins' deception.

If she'd thought she felt sick before, it had nothing on how she felt now, but now it wasn't herself she felt wretched for. All her tears were for Helena, the love-liest, kindest friend an eleven-year-old girl thrust into a brand-new overwhelming world could have wished for and whose steadfast loyalty and unconditional love had been a mainstay of her life ever since.

Just as she was about to press the button to call her back, the phone rang in her hand. It was Helena.

For a moment she was too choked to speak.

'Kate?'

Hating to hear the hoarseness in her best friend's voice, she swallowed hard. 'I'm so sorry. I've ruined everything.' And with that, she burst into tears.

'Don't cry,' Helena beseeched. 'Please, Kate, don't cry. It's not your fault. This is all on me. I begged you to find him when—'

'You *didn't*.'

'I *did*. I was so wrapped up in my own problems that

I ignored the signs that something was happening between you and sent you to him.'

'Nothing was going on before the wedding, I swear. I never meant for anything to happen.'

'I know you didn't,' Helena said softly.

'He's coming back to you today, and—'

'I can't be married to Leander, not now. Tell him to stay in California. It's a feeding frenzy here and it's going to get worse before it gets better because I can't do this any more. I'm calling a press conference. There's been so many secrets and lies and so many people hurt that I can't do it any more. I need to tell the truth and—'

Panic scratched at her throat. 'Helena, *don't*! You'll lose—'

'I *have* to. I have to put things right. I've hurt so many people.'

Kate's heart ached to hear the pain in her best friend's voice. 'You haven't. You tried so hard to do the right thing and it was for the best of reasons. I'm the one who's screwed everything up.'

'What happened was inevitable. You and Leander are meant to be together.'

She had to summon every ounce of courage to whisper the admission, 'It's over.'

There was silence down the phone then, 'Oh, my love, I'm sorry.'

Something in the way Helena said this sparked an understanding in Kate that made the ache in her heart sharpen acutely. 'Oh, Helena. Did it happen for you as well?'

A barely audible, 'Yes. And it's over too. I wasn't enough for him.'

Kate closed her eyes and sighed, wishing with all her aching heart that she could magic herself to Greece and tightly embrace the woman who was as good as a sister to her.

'Helena?' she said into the silence.

'I'm here.'

'Were the Liassidis twins born unfeeling bastards or is it something they cultivated individually as they got older?'

Helena's surprised snort of laughter triggered Kate's own laughter and though the laughter from them both was laced with a huge dollop of pain, Kate felt the better for it.

'You know what, when all this is sorted I'm going to take you up on your offer and fly out to Borneo...' A touch of alarm came into Helena's voice. 'Tell me you're still going.'

Kate sighed heavily. What else could she do? Throw away her life's plans for a selfish man who didn't want her love? 'I'm still going, and it would be the best thing ever to have you come see me there.'

'I'm not going to kiss any orangutans,' Helena warned.

'Good, because that's my job, remember?'

The silence after the next bout of laughter had a poignancy to it. It was time to say goodbye and face their individual demons.

'Are you sure you want to do this?' Kate asked.

'No, but I have to.'

'I wish I could be there to hold your hand through it.'

'I wish you could be too. Have a safe flight to Borneo.'

'I will.' She closed her eyes and said goodbye in their own language. 'Loves ya.'

'Loves ya too.'

The call ended, Kate finally got out of the car and climbed the steps onto the jet that would fly her away from Leander.

Taking her seat, she breathed in deeply and looked out of the window. The sun had fully risen and she welcomed its soft golden rays on her face. It gave her the strength she needed to make one last communication with Leander.

CHAPTER TWELVE

LEANDER FOUND A channel showing the press conference—a whole host of European channels had decided to cut their planned broadcasts short to televise it live—and tried not to look at the sofa Kate had spent her first two nights under his roof sleeping on.

While the Greek presenter gave an enthusiastic and highly speculative account of the 'Liassidis Twin Swap', Leander looked again at the message that had pinged in a short while ago.

The press know everything. Helena is going to hold a press conference and confirm the truth. Not sure when but very soon. Your husband services are no longer required. She says it's best you don't go back yet.

He thought back to that night in Athens. He'd insisted Kate store his number on her phone when they'd set off to the nightclub, just in case she became separated from the rest of them.

He cradled his head. He was still reeling from everything that had happened since the early hours. Leo's call had sent him spinning.

Theós, he'd never expected that. Leo calling. An un-expected outpouring Leander had been unprepared for.

He still couldn't get his head around it.

Strangely, there had been nothing satisfying in hearing his proud brother admit that he'd been wrong to behave the way he had. Nothing at all. Not when he had Kate's accusations about his part in their ongoing estrangement still ringing in his ears.

'Leo,' he'd said when his usually uncommunicative brother had paused for breath. 'Believe me, I appreciate what you're saying but right now isn't a good time for me. I'm sorry for dragging you into this mess and please, tell Helena that I'm sorry for letting her down.'

The silence that had followed this had been stark, reminding him that Leo had never enjoyed the easy friendship Leander had always shared with Helena. Not since Helena hit adolescence, in any case. Before then, Helena had followed them both around like a little puppy. That had been in the days when the Liassidis twins had been closer than borlotti beans from the same pod.

The only person he'd ever experienced a closeness like that with was Kate, who at that point would have been high in the air, flying away from him.

The blood whooshing in his head had increased to a roar, and he'd had to breathe deeply to cut through the silence and say, 'I need to go. When I come home, we'll talk properly. Okay?'

'Okay,' Leo had agreed slowly. 'I would like that.'

He'd swallowed a sharp pang. 'So would I.'

Now, minutes—or was it hours?—since that conversation and the magnitude of it had finally penetrated.

Leo had called him. Leo had reached out for the first time in five years. More than that, he'd reached across the divide created fourteen years ago, *truly* reached out. As a brother. As a twin. As the other half of his coin.

What had happened to his brother to make him so reflective and actually reach out and say all he'd said? Something had happened. It must have done.

So lost was he in trying to remember everything his twin had said to him that he almost missed the start of the press conference. One look at Helena's drawn face filling the screen and suddenly it became clear to him what had happened to his brother and explained the stark silence that had followed Leander's first mention of Helena's name.

Helena had happened to him.

Just like Kate had happened to Leander.

Helena's statement was short but heartfelt, taking full responsibility for the Liassidis twins' deception. When she'd finished and the audience was invited to ask questions, Leander could watch no more and turned the television off.

He rubbed the back of his neck and expelled a long breath.

It wasn't fair for Helena to take all the blame. Whatever had subsequently happened between Leo and Helena, Leo had been an unwilling party in the whole affair. Leander was the one who'd enthusiastically agreed to the deception. The blame for the whole sorry situation lay with him too.

Leander carried his surfboard across the sand and was knee-deep in the ocean before setting it down and lying on it. The pull was strong and he paddled out with spray drenching him and his board rising and falling sharply with the motion. The latent violence tugging beneath him in that early morning surf didn't faze him. He welcomed it. He needed to feel something.

He'd been numb since he'd released a written statement shortly after watching Helena's press conference. He'd kept the statement itself short.

Helena is an honourable woman who was doing the wrong thing for the right reasons. I make no excuse for my own part in the deception. Leonidas is my twin and his actions were those of a brother protecting a brother. I request that people respect his and Helena's privacy, and also the privacy of Kate Hawkins who is blameless in all of this.

He knew from his parents, who'd been unable to conceal their bewilderment at the situation, that the media frenzy hadn't abated in Greece, but his security staff had been able to assure him that Kate had arrived in Borneo without any paparazzi following her.

His Californian home was still surrounded by them. He was too numb to care.

Trying to block his thoughts off, he chased a wave that surfed him back onto the beach and then paddled back out again. The wind was picking up. The size of the waves was increasing. Adrenaline was bound to start pumping soon.

How was she getting on? His discreet calls had revealed only that she'd made it to the remote orangutan orphanage safely and without being followed. He had no way of knowing how she was settling in. If she was pleased with her accommodation. How she was finding the food. How she was finding her colleagues. How she was finding her orange orphans. How she was finding the weather.

He shook water off his face and the image of Kate's face from his retinas. He was here to surf, not to think about the woman whose heart he'd broken.

He seemed to have made it a habit to break the hearts of the people who loved him the most. And Kate did love him. Loved him enough to give up her dreams for him.

His parents loved him too. He'd broken their hearts, not by refusing to join the family business but by moving continents. His mother had understood his reasons but that didn't mitigate the hurt he'd caused by leaving so suddenly and then expecting her to psychically know he was safe and well rather than checking in more than once a week to keep her worries for him to a minimum.

A larger wave was swelling, and he chased it. Judging when the time was right, he manoeuvred his feet onto the board and stood up, spreading his body weight to keep himself balanced.

As he rode the wave, he experienced a tiny shot of

adrenaline but when the ride was over, his heart was barely pumping harder than it did at rest.

He let the swell carry him back out.

Leo loved him too and, until three days ago, Leo was the one he'd hurt the most. The price of Leander's freedom had been his brother's heart. And his own heart too.

For fourteen years he'd been the Leander he'd wanted to be. Fourteen years of living his life for his own pleasure, on his own terms, not having to consider anyone else's opinions or needs. They'd been good years in which he'd accumulated unimaginable wealth. And all to prove a point, not to Leo but to himself. To prove to himself that he didn't need Leo.

Just as Kate had intuited.

But all to prove to himself too that he didn't need Leo and that he didn't miss him when the truth was he'd missed him every minute of every day. When the truth was that he did need him.

Spotting a wave forming further out but just within his reach and paddling furiously towards it, he realised the numbness had gone. Realised it because he was suddenly acutely aware that the absence, which Leo's olive branch should have healed, had deepened into a pulsating open wound and, with it, Kate's devastated face when he'd told her to forget about him flashed before him.

The adrenaline he'd been seeking pumped hard, but it was the wrong adrenaline and at the moment he realised he'd mistimed his chase of the forming wave and instead of being on its open shoulder was in the impact zone, he saw another picture of Kate, in his Athens apartment, holding a cocktail and waving a joyful arm in the air as she sang along loudly and badly and gloriously to the music playing.

His last thought when the lip of the giant wave tipped over and slammed into him was that it had been the moment he'd fallen in love with her.

Dark eyes opened and locked onto Kate's face. She stroked the dear little head. 'You okay, little one?' she murmured.

Fingers so much like her own reached up for her.

'Just a minute longer,' she told her new charge, who'd been given the name of Mari. Mari was a two-year-old orphan who'd arrived at the orphanage the day before, three weeks after Kate's arrival. Her history was a blank canvas, the assumption being that she'd been traded as a pet and then abandoned. That was the theory seeing as she'd been found in a box on a busy street in Kota Kinabalu, a coastal city surrounded by rainforest. Mari's guardian angel had reached out to Kate's charity, who'd swung straight into action. Within days she'd arrived at the sanctuary that would nurture her and teach her all the skills needed to be let out in the rainforest proper when she became full grown. At some point the poor mite had been bitten, likely by a stray dog, and infection had set in. Kate and her team had sedated her so she could clean the infection and given her a carefully measured dose of antibiotic. Just like with human children, orangutan infants had marvellous powers of recovery and she was confident that Mari would soon be playing in the nursery with all the other infants.

Once Mari's appointed carer had carried her to the special recovery room where she would be watched continuously to ensure she didn't rip off her bandage, Kate removed her mask, helped clear up, scrubbed her hands, then set off to do her final check of the day on her other inpatients, who currently ranged in age from six months to six years. Once she was satisfied that all was well, she headed outside to where the juniors were being led back from the rainforest canopy and a day of being taught how to climb trees, forage for ants and the like, and herded into their own special clearing filled with climbing and swinging equipment. Smiling broadly at Aishah, one of the carers, who currently had one of her charges clinging to her leg rather than walk himself, Kate waved flies and mosquitoes off her face and walked over to the accommodation block.

It was only once the sights and sounds—and smells, they were unavoidable—of the orphanage had faded that her own smile faded and her mood sank.

Being around the cheeky, irrepressible orangutans always lifted her spirits. Since Kate's quarantine had ended and she'd been allowed to start work properly, she'd worked her long shifts with a smile and gratitude. In her short time there, she'd been embraced as one of the team. If melancholy grabbed her, one look at the infants playing was enough to erase it.

Every step away from the sanctuary was like a slowly deflating puncture until she reached her tiny studio apartment and her mood would be completely flat.

Other than dining in the staff canteen—the staff apartments contained only a fridge and a microwave—she had no plans for the evening. No video calls with her family. No video call with Helena.

It still made her chest go cold to remember getting off the plane in the humid Borneo heat to a call from Helena where her friend had tentatively told her about Leander's near-death experience while surfing. She'd quickly reassured her that he was recovering well with nothing more serious than a bad concussion from where his board had hit his head. It had been his good fortune that local surfers he was friendly with had seen him in the ocean and had been paddling out to join him. They'd seen immediately that he was in trouble and rescued him.

The minute that call had ended, Kate had brought up all the food she'd eaten on the plane and then physically shook for three hours.

In all their video calls since, Kate had refused outright to discuss Leander. She couldn't even bear to hear his name. Her family were forbidden from mentioning him too, or talking about Greece or California.

That evening, she had nothing to distract her from thinking about him.

She didn't *want* to think about him. She wasn't a masochist.

And she didn't want to look at the photos she'd taken of him during that wonderful week in Greece, before he'd gone cold on her. Despite knowing how unhealthy it was, the first thing she did once she'd trudged up the wooden steps and stepped into her apartment was curl up on the decades-old sofa and bring the pictures up.

It was a pattern she'd followed every working day since her arrival.

It didn't matter how much her head told her to follow Leander's advice and forget about him, her heart refused to let go. That was just a sad fact. As another sad fact of her life had been that to get the grades she'd needed meant working harder than everyone else, she knew the only way for her heart to let go and reach acceptance that she would never see him again was to work hard at it.

After scrolling blindly backwards and forwards through pictures of his gorgeous face for a good twenty minutes, she took a deep breath and straightened herself.

It was time.

She would never forget him if she had these photos as a constant reminder.

She brought the first picture up, a selfie of Kate, Helena and Leander leaning against the car he'd collected her from the airport in. Delete.

The next photo was another selfie. The three of them around the Liassidis family swimming pool. Delete.

The next was just Leander. He was walking towards Kate carrying a pitcher of sangria that she'd cheekily requested. The camera had captured the magnificence of his body and that devastating smile. Delete.

One by one, all the images of the man who'd turned his back on her love were erased. By the time she'd finished, the screen of her phone was soaked with tears and her heart was shredded.

It was a long time before she was able to bring herself to head to the canteen for her first meal of the day. Because that was something else she needed to work at. Eating. Her work clothes were already loose. She didn't have enough body fat on her to lose any more weight. She would force her appetite to come out of hibernation.

And she would let go of Leander.

Leander had travelled all over the world. He'd climbed mountains, skied mountains and trekked the Gobi Desert. Those were just the things he remembered off the top of his head. Even with the things that didn't immediately spring to mind, he had never been in an environment like this. Never felt the humidity actually soak into his skin. When they reached a huge clearing at the edge of the rainforest and he got out of the truck that had collected him from the airport, the noises assaulted his ears.

A tiny, formidable-looking woman with salt-and-pepper hair steamed over to him.

'Mr Liassidis?' she said in perfect English that contained only the trace of an accent and not the slightest trace of warmth.

'Call me Leander,' he said, extending his hand. 'You must be Yuna.' The woman who ran the orphanage.

She ignored his hand. 'That's me. Your documents.'

Prepared, he handed everything over. He would have been here weeks sooner if the concussion from his mistimed surf and then bureaucracy, not from the Malaysian government but the charity itself, hadn't held him up. This orphanage was too precious for them to risk allowing shortcuts of any kind. Only a sizeable donation had got the trustees onside. Yuna had been vocal in her resentment of his special treatment. If Leander wanted to see a member of her staff, then he should make private arrangements to meet at the house in a local town the staff used on their weekends off. As she'd then refused to tell him when Kate's weekend off was, he'd gone through every expected hoop to get this far.

Unhappily satisfied all was in order, she started walking. 'Remember, you must not enter any building our charges are in.'

Even though the sun was falling, there were plenty of workers around, all going about their business, and he followed Yuna past buildings of varying sizes that all buzzed with life and activity. If he wasn't feeling so sick with nerves, he'd find it fascinating.

The orphanage's buildings behind them, they followed a narrow path until they reached what looked like a low, wide temple.

'Wait here,' Yuna commanded. 'I shall see if she wants to see you.'

Leander clamped his lips together and gave a short nod. That had been one of Yuna's many conditions. If Kate refused to see him, he would be escorted straight back to the truck.

Yuna disappeared around the side of the building and returned tight-faced.

His heart plunged. 'She won't see me?'

She shook her head. 'No, she wasn't in.'

The relief almost knocked him off his feet.

'She must be eating. Come.' And she set off again.

CHAPTER THIRTEEN

KATE SWIRLED NOODLES around her fork and, ignoring the expectant faces of two of her colleagues barely suppressing their laughter, popped it in her mouth. The chilli heat this time was instant.

Mouth on fire, she finished her glass of milk. 'You two are evil,' she seethed, only half joking.

Her photograph deleting spree meant she'd been the last to arrive in the canteen. The only main course left was the noodles with chicken and prawns and peanuts, which was absolutely delicious excepting the abundance of Thai chillies infused in it.

'More milk?' Stefan, the only other European who worked there, asked.

'Bring the cow,' she laughed, and added another forkful into her mouth.

So much for her not being a masochist!

But this was good. A little companionship and conversation and laughter. The days here were long and people rarely lingered after dinner, most grabbing their needed sleep. The nature of their jobs meant a full night's sleep wasn't guaranteed. Kate was looking forward to her first weekend off and the promise of a sightseeing trip with one of the nurses. Anything to fill her days and keep her brain busy. Stop her mind from taking over.

The main door opened and Yuna, Kate's slightly terrifying boss, walked in. She clocked Kate and zoomed over to her.

'You have a visitor.'

Kate stared at her blankly.

'A visitor,' Yuna repeated, this time more slowly. 'Shall I let him in? Or kick his ass back to the airport?'

Him?

Her stare zipped to the door ten feet from where she was sitting.

Standing at the threshold…

She shoved her chair back with such force it would have toppled if the wall hadn't been there to break its fall.

Leander knew he was breaking the cardinal rule. Yuna had been explicit. He must let Yuna ask Kate privately if she was willing to see him.

His legs had disobeyed before his brain realised what they were doing, and the first thing he'd seen looming through the opened door was Kate sitting with two men whose company she was clearly enjoying.

To see her animated face in the flesh after all this time had sucker-punched him.

It was the face he'd seen when he'd come round from

his near drowning on the beach and known in that instant that he'd made the biggest mistake of his life.

The animation had fallen the instant she'd spotted Leander.

Yuna followed the direction of Kate's now-ashen face. Features contorted with fury, she pointed a finger at him. '*You*. Do *not* move.'

To Kate she asked, 'Well?'

The two men Kate had been seated with had also risen and were flanking Kate and the diminutive boss, staring at Leander with the deepest suspicion. As they were barely taller than the women, the sight of them geeing themselves to square up to him would have been comical if he'd been focusing on anything but the face he'd missed more than it was possible to believe.

Forcing his body to remain at the threshold, he asked hoarsely, 'Can we talk?'

Talk, Kate thought dazedly. Leander wanted to talk. That was if it even was him. Wasn't it known that too high a dose of chillies could make a person hallucinate? It wasn't actually possible that the figure standing in the canteen doorway was Leander. People didn't just turn up here. This was a rainforest, for goodness' sake!

He'd told her to forget him.

'Can I kick him out or not?' Yuna asked impatiently.

Even though she knew this wasn't happening, Kate shook her head, at the same time grabbing Yuna's skinny wrist to keep herself anchored and hoarsely whispering, 'Please stay.'

The noodles she'd been eating were churning in her stomach, clashing with the violence of her heartbeats.

'You hear that?' Yuna taunted. 'She wants me to stay. So get on with it.'

There was something strangely reassuring in Yuna's protective stance and in the body language of the two men with them. Leander wouldn't allow himself to hope that he had a future with Kate. If he left Borneo with her deserved rejection ringing in his ears then at least he would have the comfort of knowing she was amongst people who would care and look out for her.

He had to clear his throat and then clear it again.

'Kate, I'm sorry. I'm here to beg you, on bended knee if that's what it takes for you to take me back.'

Even with the distance between them, he heard the whimper that came from her closed mouth. It was a sound that sliced through his heart.

'Since you've been gone…' He shook his head and breathed deeply. He could never explain in mere words the hole that existed in him. And then he sighed and filled his lungs with more of the humid air. 'I say *since you've been gone* but you only went because I pushed you away, and I pushed you away because I'm the biggest fool on this earth. I knew you were the best thing that had ever happened to me. I was too stupid to admit it to myself but deep in here…' He made a fist and pressed it to his heart. 'I knew I loved you.'

Her eyes widened.

'What I didn't know was that living without you would be such torture. It's a torture I deserve. I've hurt you so many times and all because I was too damned stubborn—and frightened—to accept that the life I'd built around my own needs and pleasures was crumbling around me. It started crumbling the moment you first jumped into the back of my car on the island and now it's nothing but ruins.'

Her hand fluttered to her mouth.

'I've always been selfish, Kate,' he admitted starkly, wishing he could peer deep into her brain and see what she was thinking. 'But you already know that. You've already accepted that. You see me exactly as I am and still you love me... Loved me.' He swallowed a lump that had lodged itself in his throat. 'You are the only person in the world I can't be selfish with. Your happiness is all that matters to me. You don't make me want to be a better man; I have no choice in it. To hurt you is to hurt myself. Since you've been gone…since I pushed you away,' he corrected himself, then grabbed the back of his head, trying desperately to find the words he needed to say before the fear gripping his heart and lungs took full control of him. 'Everything you said about my estrangement with Leo was true. I functioned for fourteen years without him and it's only now that he's back in my life that I can acknowledge just how badly I missed him in those years.' He attempted a smile. 'What you said about us being identically stubborn is also true.'

One of the first things Leander had done when he'd come round after his surfing accident was call his brother and apologise properly for the first time for leaving the way he had all those years ago and for being a selfish coward in the way he'd gone about leaving. With Leo insisting the blame lay with him and being adamant the deterioration of their relationship after the family business trouble was his fault, while Leander saw clearly now that it was his fault and that he should have gone home and insisted his brother lean on him for emotional support, the twins had been forced to agree that they had both played their part in the whole sorry mess and that it was the future that mattered now. A future as brothers. Twin brothers.

Who cared if people couldn't tell them apart? The one person who mattered most knew with one glance that he was Leander. She saw *him*.

Soon, once everything with Kate was resolved for good or for ill, Leander would fly to his brother and they would sit down for the first time in too many years and share a beer together. Whether he would be able to taste the beer and take enjoyment in his brother's company all depended on what came next now.

'I could function without Leo, but I can't function without you. I don't just miss you, Kate.' Something hot was stabbing the back of his eyes. 'The world still turns but it turns without me, because without you in my life, there is nothing for me. My life belongs to you. I love you and I don't know how to live without you. I...' His voice cracked as suddenly it hit him that he really could walk out of this place and never see her again. That Kate, his beautiful, joyful, funny pixie princess might have already moved on emotionally.

That he'd hurt her too deeply for her to be able to put her trust in him again.

He would have no one to blame but himself.

Kate had listened to Leander's almost rambling speech with the sensation that she'd stepped out of her body and was watching weightless from above, only her grip on Yuna's wrist stopping her from floating up to the sky. It had been all too incredible, and even as she'd listened to every word he said, a dazed voice had kept repeating in her ear that it couldn't be him.

It was the break in his voice that pulled her back down to the ground. A break that speared straight into her heart, and suddenly she saw him clearly. Leander.

Her Leander, the man who had lit her heart from that very first smile and switched on unimaginable passions and joy and a zest in her veins that had all dimmed into nothing without him.

Her Leander, looking utterly wrecked.

He'd lost weight. That wasn't stubble around his jaw but a thick, unruly black beard. His hair looked like it hadn't ever seen a comb. His eyes were those of a man who'd lost the ability to sleep.

Those eyes shone with tears.

Those eyes shone with agony.

Staring into them…

She saw it. The truth. It was right there, his heart shining through his tortured stare.

Leander had come to her.

There was a gentle push on her back. She didn't need it, or know or care who'd done it and didn't look to see. Her gaze was glued in its entirety to the man her heart had gift-wrapped itself for long before her head had realised it.

She walked to him with that floating sensation drifting through her again.

Leander couldn't breathe. Couldn't speak. Couldn't hear anything above the roar of noise in his head. Couldn't tear his gaze from the figure walking like a dream towards him. Diamond stud earrings glittered in her ears...

She reached him.

Her throat moved. Her chin wobbled. A tear spilled down her cheek.

For the longest time neither of them spoke.

Her throat moved again, and then her chest rose and fell like a sigh, and she put a trembling palm to his bearded cheek and quiveringly whispered, 'If you ever push me away again or run from me then I will rip your heart out with my hands.'

A scintilla of the weight compressing his lungs lifted.

Covering the hand against his cheek tightly, he nuzzled into it. 'Take it now. It's yours.'

Jade eyes fixed on his, she cupped the back of his neck with her other hand. 'For ever?'

He almost closed his eyes at the rush of emotions her touch on his neck evoked, but he kept his stare locked on hers, willing her to read the sincerity in them. 'It's yours, Kate, for as long as you want it.'

The tiniest curve tugged at the side of her mouth. 'I want it for ever.'

'You have it. My heart and my soul.' The soul she'd saved without even trying.

Faces inching closer, her stare bore into his for what seemed an eternity before the curve widened a little bit more and he felt it, felt Kate's heart and soul reaching out to meet his and fuse together, lifting the weight inside him in its entirety.

'I love you,' Kate breathed as their mouths brushed together, and as she was pulled into the deepest, sweetest and yet most passionate kiss of her life, the last shreds of her heart flew back together and knitted seamlessly into place, leaving her whole.

He loved her. Leander loved her.

An unsubtle cough behind them broke their mouths apart.

They'd both forgotten they had an audience.

Not loosening their hold on each other, they locked eyes again. Overwhelmed by all the emotion flowing through her, still only half believing that all this was really happening, that Leander did love her and that he'd come all this way for her, Kate giggled and tightened her grip around his neck. 'I love you,' she repeated.

'And I love you. Always, always.'

The unsubtle cough sounded again. 'I suppose this means I'm going to have to advertise for a new vet,' Yuna grumbled.

'Absolutely not,' Leander said firmly before Kate could even think what to answer. 'Kate will stay here for as long as she wants to be here. I'll be making the changes necessary to make our marriage work.'

Kate's eyebrows lifted like a shot. 'Marriage?'

'If you'll have me.'

If she'd have him? In the space of a few hours Kate had gone from rock bottom to feeling that she'd been lifted to the top of the world.

Smiling so widely her muscles screamed in protest, she kissed him with a passion so deep it left him in no doubt what her answer was.

EPILOGUE

THERE'S A GREEK ISLAND, only a short hop from the Liassidis family's island, that's a mecca for travellers of all varieties. A long stretch of its golden beach is entirely private but at its border with the public beach sits a wooden shack with an open front and outside tables.

Tourists and locals alike have learned that the best months to visit Kate's Cocktail Bar are May and June, when its gregarious owner can be found behind the bar welcoming familiar faces and strangers as old friends. His wife, the eponymous Kate, is a regular presence in those months too, although she leaves the cocktail-making to her husband. Come the end of June, the couple fly out to Borneo, where they spend six months living in a bespoke treetop house in the sprawling grounds that constitutes the orangutan orphanage his non-cocktail-making wife works at. Every year, a week before Christmas, they fly back to Europe to visit their respective families, often bringing them all together in their magnificent Greek villa, before they move on to California, where the husband enjoys weeks of surfing and his wife pretends her heart isn't in her throat every time he carries his board to the beach. February, March and April are spent wherever they fancy it.

It's a semi-nomadic life Kate absolutely adores but one that must soon come to an end, and with excitement and a tiny bit of nerves sloshing in her stomach, she wanders out of the villa in search of her husband. It's a short search.

He's sitting on a wooden stool at the bar of Kate's Cocktail Bar scribbling on a napkin. Music's already playing. It's still a little early for even the hardened drinkers, and his concentration is such that at first he doesn't hear her approach. When he does, the wide, beaming smile that's entirely for her lights his face.

He pulls her between his legs, squeezes her bottom and kisses her as if they were still newlyweds. She has no doubt they will always kiss like newlyweds. And then he must see something on her face for his eyebrows draw together in question.

She grins.

A moment later he understands what the grin means and an almost dazed smile comes close to splitting his face.

The front of the shack's shutters are closed so they can celebrate the life they've created together in private.

Their lives will have to change again.

Neither of them has any doubt that they will make it work.

They always make it work.

* * * * *